ALLERGIC
TO MY FAMILY

ALLERGIC
TO MY FAMILY

Liza Ketchum Murrow

Holiday House / New York

Library of Congress Cataloging-in-Publication Data
Murrow, Liza Ketchum, 1946–
Allergic to my family : a novel / by Liza Ketchum Murrow.
p.   cm.
Summary: Living with five brothers and sisters, a pet skunk, and
two nutty parents, fourth grader Rosie sometimes feels that her
family is too busy to appreciate her.
ISBN 0-8234-0959-7
[1. Family life—Fiction.] I. Title.
PZ7.M96713AI   1992   91-31529   CIP   AC
[Fic]—dc20

For my favorite big family:
Tom and Polly,
Dylan, Diana, Ben, Bray, and Freddy—
with love

CONTENTS

INTRODUCING
ROSIE MAXWELL

I always knew my family was crazy, but I never dreamed it could get any worse—until the night Mama and Dad made their big announcement. That's when I realized we'd gone over the edge. Pretty soon, I figured, the Maxwell family of Copper Canyon, California, would be wilder than a Santa Ana windstorm, and as far as I could see, no one cared but me.

It all started in February, just after I turned nine. We were having what my parents call a "normal" dinner: Silas had spilled his milk twice, Katie complained every two seconds about the slippery mushrooms in the sauce, Shirley talked to Mama like there was no one else at the table, and Dan kept glancing at the floor, trying to read his book while he was eating.

"Can I be excused?" I asked, picking up my plate. I wanted to run outside and practice the back flip we'd just learned in gymnastics, but Dad said, "Hold it, Rosie—everyone else, stay where you are a minute.

3

Your mother and I have a special surprise for you.''

He grinned at Mama, and that's when I started getting this itchy feeling in my scalp like something was up. My parents had goofy, lopsided grins, and they were holding hands. Even Shirley, who usually acts like she knows everything, looked suspicious.

''Don't tell me,'' Shirley said.

I hadn't caught on yet. ''What?'' I asked. ''Tell us. Dan, do you know what the secret is?''

Dan scooped up his book before he glanced at me. ''Huh?'' he mumbled. I swear, he reads even when he's sleeping. No wonder Dad calls him ''The Professor.''

''A secret?'' Katie yelped, clutching the table. ''What is it?''

Silas sat very still, listening, and the rest of us held our breath while Dad took off his glasses and wiped them on his sleeve. He always does that when he's nervous. ''Your mother and I want you to know that our family will be a little bigger in June.''

Shirley pursed her lips and whistled. ''A new baby,'' she said. ''No wonder.''

''No wonder what?'' Mama asked, looking puzzled.

''No wonder you've been wearing Dad's old shirts lately,'' Shirley said.

For a second, I was glued to my seat. Then I dropped my plate and jumped up, tipping my chair over. ''*Six kids*!'' I screeched. ''You've got to be kidding.''

"Rosie," Dad said, rubbing his beard, "tone it down."

"Wait!" I yelled. "You guys are *nuts*. I mean, no one has that many kids anymore!"

"Then I guess that makes us original," Mama said in this sleepy, faraway kind of voice. "Anyway, I think even numbers are nice, don't you?"

"I've got to call Patsy," Shirley said, jumping up. "She won't believe this."

"Great," I said, "tell everyone in Los Angeles, why don't you?"

I waited for Mama and Dad to say something. Ever since Shirley turned twelve, she'd practically *lived* on the phone. Didn't they care that she was broadcasting family secrets to the whole universe? I guess not, because they just beamed at her, and the rest of us, as if we were the most ordinary family in the world. I looked around the table. "Dan, don't you think this is *insane*?"

Dan held his finger on the page of his book. "I don't know," he said and started reading again. Silas frowned, but of course he didn't say anything.

Katie bounced on her chair until her black braids went up and down like Yo-Yos. "A baby—Silas, maybe they'll have twins again!" she squealed.

That was the worst idea I'd ever heard. "Isn't one set enough?" I asked. I still remember when they were born, almost four years ago, and Dad announced,

"Well, folks, guess what—we got two for the price of one."

Mama laughed. "We're only having one baby this time," she said. "We checked that out. And it's our last, don't worry."

But I *was* worried. "Go ahead, have it," I said. "But don't expect *me* to change its diapers." I stomped outside, slamming the kitchen door. Really, anyone who's dumb enough to have six kids, when they already have five, had better plan on cleaning up their own messes.

After that, it seemed like we didn't talk about anything except babies. Shirley begged to go shopping for baby clothes, even though Mama said we had plenty of stuff left over from the twins. Katie stuck her hand under Mama's loose shirt every day to see if she could feel the baby kick. Silas drew pictures of a woman with a wriggly fish inside her belly, while Dan read us weird names from this library book called *Naming Your Baby*. Didn't anyone realize we were going to be in a big mess—very soon?

One day, when we were all crammed into the station wagon to go shopping, I had a terrible thought. "Where's it going to sleep?" I asked.

Mama glanced at me in the rearview mirror. "The baby? It will sleep with us at first, when it's still waking up in the night," she said. "Then we'll see."

We'll see. Those are dangerous words. "What do you mean?" I asked.

"Well, it depends whether it's a boy or a girl."

Just what I was afraid of. "If you put it in our room, I'm moving to the couch," I announced.

"Great," Shirley said, with this sugary smile. "Maybe she'll be the kind of sister who puts her stuff away in the cupboards."

I ignored her. I was waiting for Mama to say: "Don't worry, you won't have to share your room," but she kept right on driving. I squirmed in my seat. This was worse than I thought. I glanced around the station wagon. "Where will the baby sit when we go on drives?" I asked. "On the roof?" I pointed at Shirley and Dan sitting beside me, then at Katie and Silas, squinched into the jump seat. "Look, there's no more space right now."

Mama and Dad glanced at each other like they hadn't even thought of it. "Good point," Dad said. "I guess we'll deal with that problem when the time comes."

I sighed. "Most parents would figure out if there was room for a baby *before* they had one," I said.

"There's always room for another baby," Dad said. "And that's enough complaints, Rosie Maxwell." His chin stuck out and his beard quivered the way it does when he gets mad, but I wasn't done yet.

"What about gymnastics?" I demanded.

"What about them?" Mama sighed, pulling into the parking lot.

"Who will take me to gymnastics class when the baby comes?"

"I will." Dad's voice sounded tired. "Or we can carpool. Don't worry, Ms. Gymnast, we'll get you there."

I crossed my arms tight across my chest. Dad could make fun of me now, but just wait a few years. I'd have the last laugh when I vaulted into a handspring full twist, right in front of the Olympic judges, and pulled a perfect score.

We piled out of the car and into the supermarket, filling the center aisle with kids and carts.

"My, my, I see you have the whole family out," an old lady said to Dad.

"That's right," he said. "It's quite a crew. And we're adding one more, in June."

The old lady raised her eyebrows. "Really? Will that make it five now, or six?"

"Six," I said loudly. And then, under my breath, I muttered, "Six, six, oughta get their heads fixed."

The lady reached out, and before I had time to jump, she put her hand on my curls as if I were a pet dog. "Wonder if the new baby will have hair like this one?" She looked at Dad's shiny bald head, at Mama, with her long, black braid, then at the rest of us. "Funny, he's the only one with those curls."

He? I was so mad I could hardly talk. "I'm not a he, I'm a *she*!" I stomped to the front of the store, blinking my eyes fast to keep from crying, and plunked myself down on the bench near the cash registers. Who was that old lady anyway? She should talk about hair—hers looked like she'd dipped it in blue paint. Besides, could I help it if my hair was so curly it was beyond frizz? Bromjay, the star creep in my school, told me once I looked like a lion with a bad perm.

I sat there boiling mad until my family came stumbling down the aisles with two carts that were so overloaded you could hardly tell who was pushing them. When Dad and Shirley got in line, other people wheeled their carts to different registers; no one wanted to get stuck behind us.

Mama saw me on the bench and came over to sit down. Her belly was getting big; she rested her hands on it like a table.

"Why'd that lady call me a boy?" I demanded. "Couldn't she see my earrings?"

Mama put her arm around me. "I guess not—anyway, some boys have them now."

"Not in both ears," I said.

Mama gave me a little squeeze. "You look like a girl to me. I'm sure she didn't mean to hurt your feelings. If it really bothers you, you could wear a skirt."

Of course, Mama knew I wouldn't do that. Why should I give up handstands, cartwheels, and flips just because some kooky lady called me a boy?

I pulled away from Mama and studied her face. "How come I'm the only one who doesn't look like you or Dad?"

"What do you mean?" Mama asked.

"Look at them," I said, pointing to the checkout counter. "Silas and Dan have blue eyes and the same color hair as Dad."

Mama smiled. "Your Dad doesn't *have* much hair, ladybug."

"I'm *not* a bug," I said. "How about you and Shirley and Katie? You all have black hair and eyes."

Mama squinted at me. "You take after your dad a little bit," she said. "Of course, it might be the glasses—"

"Gee, thanks," I said, standing up and glaring at her. "Maybe if I grow a beard, people will think I'm Dad's twin."

"Now Rosie," Mama said, but I ignored her and ran out the door. I'm just a misfit, I thought, kicking an empty soda can around the parking lot. Ms. Fit. It sounded like some mean teacher's name. I thought about Mama's belly getting bigger and bigger and decided I had only one last hope—that when the new baby was born, it might look like me. Otherwise, I'd always be the odd one out.

PART I
SILENT SILAS

1. The Trouble with Silas

When Clara finally arrived in June, I checked her out pretty carefully. Dad took us to the hospital one at a time, and when it was my turn, Mama pulled me up on the bed beside her. Clara was sleeping in Mama's lap, wrapped in a soft cotton blanket. "Isn't she dear?" Mama asked.

I pulled the cloth away from her head. I didn't tell Mama, but I'd been wishing something might be wrong with her so I wouldn't be the only oddball in the family. But Clara looked like most babies. Her face was red and scaly, her wrinkled neck smelled like old laundry, and she had ten toes and fingers; I counted them. Plus, she was as bald as a cucumber.

"When will her hair grow?" I asked Mama.

Mama stroked Clara's head. "Not for a while. You were bald for months, before your curls started to sprout."

Me, with no hair? That was hard to believe. Still,

there was a chance Clara's hair might get curly when it came in. But when my grandmother, Dad's mom, came to help out, she took away my last little shreds of hope. She held Clara on her lap, studied her face, and then looked around at the rest of us.

"A darling baby," Grandmother announced. "The spitting image of Shirley and Katie."

I knew what that meant. Clara would grow up looking beautiful like Mama and my sisters, leaving me the odd girl out.

Pretty soon, I had other things to worry about. For the first few weeks, all Clara did was cry, and her screech was louder than the whole family yelling at once. Even with the pillow jammed over my head, I could hear her bawling in Mama and Dad's room, right on the other side of the wall. Sometimes I dragged my sleeping bag downstairs to the couch, but it was lumpy and uncomfortable there—plus, Clara's screams still hurt my ears from that far away. The whole family got more and more grumpy and cross. Even Katie, who loves other people's babies, asked if we could give Clara away to the old lady at the supermarket.

"It's too noisy here," I told my dad one morning. "I think I should go to gymnastics camp."

Dad didn't answer. He just stood by the kitchen window drinking coffee and staring outside. "You stay there for two weeks," I went on. (Was he listening?) "My gym teacher told me about it."

Dad pushed his glasses onto the end of his nose. They were all steamed up. "Dream on, Rosie," he said finally.

"What's wrong with a dream?" I asked. "Besides, then you'd only have five kids to take care of. It would be easier."

Dad shook his head. "It's too expensive, hon. Maybe next year."

I'd heard *that* one before. I begged him and Mama a few more times, but pretty soon it was July and I was trudging back and forth to the same old boring day camp I'd been to every summer since kindergarten, with nothing to look forward to but gymnastics once a week. Dan was old enough to go to camp with me this year, but he wasn't much company; he sang weird songs to himself or read street signs the whole way there and back.

One afternoon when Dan and I came home, the yard was quiet. The swings were empty; so was the sandbox. Silas was riding his Big Wheel trike up and down the sidewalk, pedaling as fast as he could, but no one else was around.

"Where's Mama?" I asked him.

Silas pointed at the house. I ran up the path and into the kitchen. Everything was quiet—too quiet. There was a note from Mama to Dad on the counter. "I'm in my studio," it said. "Please pick up Shirley at 4. Katie's at Marney's house."

Gee, thanks, I thought. No welcome home note for me or Dan? Maybe Mama had forgotten about us.

I drank some milk and wandered down the hall to the living room. Katie's stuffed animals were all over the floor, and my dad was snoring on the couch, holding Clara on his chest. When Clara was born, Mama said it was nice she came in the summer, when my dad didn't have to teach. As far as I could see, all he'd done was yawn or take naps since school was out, and I didn't see how *that* was such a help.

Boring, boring, boring, I thought. You'd think if you had five brothers and sisters, you could find someone to play with. But Dan had already disappeared, probably to find a book or study some bizarre insect in the bushes.

I tiptoed down the path to the garage, where Mama did her painting and drawing. I knew she wouldn't like it if I interrupted her, but maybe she wouldn't be working too hard today.

I peeked in. Mama was sound asleep with her head on her drawing table and a lamp shining in her face. She looked peaceful, even though her cheek was resting in a little glob of orange paint. I went back down the path, walked on my hands across the grass, did a flip and sat on the curb watching Silas roar down the sidewalk.

He zoomed past, making a motorcycle noise. "Hey, Silas!" I yelled. "Talk to me."

But of course he didn't. That was the trouble with Silas. He couldn't talk, even though he was almost four years old. Never mind that other kids learned to talk when they were two or three at the most. Silas had to be different. Of course, he was good at making all kinds of weird noises. He could squeal like a fire engine, roar like a train, or make a chop-chop noise like a helicopter. But words? Forget it. He didn't know any.

"Hey, Silas," I called as he pedaled past, "what are you doing?"

Silas's forehead almost touched the plastic handle bars and his wispy hair hung over his eyes. He looked up at me, waved, and then went, "Brrrrrrr!" like an engine warming up. His chubby legs churned around, and the plastic wheels rattled louder than a real car.

Another one who's not like me, I thought. Then suddenly I had an idea. Of course—why didn't I think of it before? Silas might not look like me or act like me, but maybe if I could get him to talk, I'd find out he was *thinking* like me.

Silas wheeled his trike into the yard, left it under the eucalyptus tree, and hurried to the patio.

"Hey, Silas," I called, running up the walk after him. "Wait for me." I was going so fast I almost stepped on Dan; he was sitting on the front steps, reading a comic.

"Guess what, Dan," I said. "I'm going to teach Silas how to talk."

Dan actually stopped reading and looked up. "Really?" he asked. "Can I help?"

"Sure," I said, even though I didn't have the faintest idea how to do it. "Come on, let's follow him." We tiptoed down the hall to Silas and Katie's room, whispering so we wouldn't wake Dad.

"Today's the perfect day to work with Silas," I said softly. "Katie's at a friend's house, and Shirley's at art class. We'll have him all to ourselves."

Silas sidled past us carrying a big cement truck and went out to the patio. In a few seconds, we heard him making a whirring, cement mixer noise. "If he does all those sounds, why can't he say words?" Dan asked.

I shrugged. "How should I know? Look at Mama and Dad; they can't figure it out either." Which was the truth. Whenever I asked them what was wrong with Silas, they always said, "Silas is perfectly normal. He'll talk when he's ready." What if he wasn't ready until he was eighteen? Or worse, what if he didn't talk when he was old enough to come to my school? The more I thought about it, the more I realized I'd better get this thing settled now. After all, Mama and Dad were obviously too busy with Clara to pay any attention to Silas. Good grief, today they even went to sleep and left him playing alone on the sidewalk!

Dan and I went into the twins' room and picked out

some books. Since Mama illustrated picture books for little kids, we always had heaps of them around the house. Dan and I carried a big stack outside. Silas was funneling sand into his cement mixer.

"Hey, Silas, want to read a book?" I asked. He shook his head and kept on playing. I found his favorite book about big machines and opened it to a picture of a cement truck. "Look, Silas," I said, poking it under his nose. "Here's one just like yours. Say 'mixer.' " I said it slowly and carefully, like a first-grade teacher helping someone read. Silas nodded and smiled, but he didn't say anything.

"What's this, Silas?" I asked, pointing to a picture of a garbage truck. "Say 'garbage truck.' "

Silas made a loud grinding noise just like the truck that picks up our trash.

"Here, let's try this one," Dan said. He picked up my mom's new pop-up book. Every page unfolded into an animal, and the words described their sounds. At the end of the book, the animals screeched and cawed and bleated together just like my dad's band at the high school. We liked the elephant page best; its long nose poked out of the book and flapped in the air.

"Elephant," said Dan, holding his finger under the words. " 'The elephant bellows like a trumpet,' " he read. "Say 'el-e-phant,' Silas."

Silas puckered his lips and made a loud, trumpeting sound. I shook my head. "This isn't going to work,"

I said. "We're going to take Silas to the doctor."
Silas's eyes got big and round.

"Why?" Dan asked, squinting at Silas. "Is he
sick?"

"Maybe there's something in his throat that keeps
him from talking. Mama and Dad should have taken
him ages ago, but they've been too busy. If Dr. Crosby
finds out what's the matter, they'll be really happy.
Come on, let's go quickly, before they wake up."

2. Dr. Crosby

I thought Silas would refuse, but he skipped right along between us all the way to the end of our canyon. I made Silas and Dan stop and look both ways at every curb, and I wasn't nervous until we opened the doctor's door. I'd never been there without my parents. Would they let us in?

But Dr. Crosby's nurse smiled when she saw us. "Rosie Maxwell—how nice to see you! Hi, Silas. Hello, Dan. How's that new baby of yours?"

"She's fine," I said quickly. The waiting room was empty, thank goodness. Silas went right to the blocks, and I whispered to the nurse, "Silas needs to see the doctor."

The nurse looked at the book on her desk. "Did your mother call for an appointment?"

I shook my head. "She's too busy."

The nurse put her hand on the phone. "We don't usually see children your age without their parents. Why don't I give her a call."

I didn't know what to say. Dan yanked on my arm. "Let's go home," he whispered, but just then Dr. Crosby opened her office door, said good-bye to a teenage boy, and peered into the waiting room.

"Why Rosie Maxwell," she said. "How are you?" She looked around. "Are your parents here?"

I shook my head. "They couldn't come." Then I said softly, "Silas needs to see you."

The nurse started to protest, but Dr. Crosby smiled. "I've got a minute. Bring him in."

"Come on, Silas," I said. We went through the little gate and down the hall to Dr. Crosby's office. There were pictures on the walls that kids had made for her, including one of mine from when I was five years old and thought bugs had at least fifty legs.

Dr. Crosby closed the door and pointed to the stool next to the tall table where kids sit to be examined. "Can you climb up there, Silas?" she asked. Silas scrambled up and perched on the edge. Dr. Crosby looked at Silas, then at me. "He looks very healthy," she said. "What's the trouble?"

"He can't talk," I said.

Dr. Crosby folded her arms and nodded. "I see." She took a deep breath. "Your parents and I have discussed this. But we'll have another look, just to make sure."

I stared at my feet. I should have known Mama and

Dad had talked to her already. If they'd only tell *me* things. But Dr. Crosby didn't seem to think it was weird that we'd brought Silas. She shone her little light in his ears, then looked in his throat for a long time. She hit his knees with a rubber hammer until they bounced, and she listened to his chest. Then she patted his head.

"You're fit as a fiddle, Silas. Hop down. We'll play Simon Says. Rosie can be the leader."

I stared. Whoever heard of a doctor playing nursery school games? Maybe our family's craziness was catching. "Give us some tricky ones," Dr. Crosby whispered in my ear. "See if you can get him to say something."

I cleared my throat. "Simon says, touch your toes," I said.

Silas, Dan, and Dr. Crosby touched their toes. I noticed that Dr. Crosby's toenail polish matched her red sandals.

"Simon says, roar like a tiger," I said.

Silas, Dr. Crosby, and Dan all made loud growling noises.

"Say your names," I said.

No one said a word.

"You should have said 'Simon says' with that one, too," Dan whispered.

How could I be so dumb, I wondered, but Dr. Crosby smiled. "Well, Rosie," she said, "Silas certainly understands everything. I think you'll just have to be patient. He'll talk when he's ready."

That night, dinner was so zooey I decided my parents probably liked having at least one kid who kept quiet. I looked around the table. Everyone was talking at once, grabbing for food, and asking questions. My parents were in outer space. Mama wiped up spilled spaghetti sauce while she stared at the wall. Dad walked around and around the table like a slow horse on a merry-go-round, bouncing Clara and humming to himself.

"Excuse me," I said, being polite for once. "Is anybody listening?"

No one was. "Ms. Crenshaw said I was ready to learn about perspective in drawing," Shirley announced, wiping her mouth with her napkin.

Miss Priss, I thought. I banged on the table and yelled, "Quiet!" All the dishes rattled. Katie jumped and Clara screamed.

"Rosie," my dad said, in his tight voice that means business. "Not so loud." He jostled Clara up and down.

"Sorry," I said, "but listen. I know why Silas can't talk."

"Don't embarrass him," Shirley hissed, but Mama actually noticed me for the first time in weeks.

"Why, honey?" she asked.

"It's because everyone else is always gabbing. Maybe if we're all quiet a minute, he'd have a chance to say something."

Dan and Katie sat still. Mama leaned toward Silas, her head cocked to the side. Dad rocked Clara back and forth until she stopped fussing. Even Shirley pursed her lips.

Silas's ears got pink. Finally Katie whispered, "He doesn't want to say anything."

I crossed my arms tight over my chest. "How do you know?"

Katie blinked her long, fluttery eyelashes. "I just do," she said softly. She looked at Silas. "He wants a piece of corn," she said.

I stared at Silas. "Do you?" I asked. He nodded, and I held up the bowl. "Say please," I said, when he reached for it.

His mouth trembled, and Katie whispered, "Please, can Silas have the corn?"

"No!" I yelled. "If you always talk for him, he'll never learn. Mama, make him say please."

Silas put his hands over his ears, and Katie started to cry.

"That's mean!" Shirley complained, and grabbed the corn, handing it to Silas. "Here, honey," she said in her sickening, fake sweet voice.

"You do everything for him," I complained.

"Rosie!" my dad roared. "This is not the time or the place to give Silas a speech lesson!"

So Silas got his corn even though he hadn't said anything. "Silent Silas, Silent Silas," I teased when no one else was listening. Two big tears rolled down his cheeks, and then I felt bad. It didn't make sense. If he understood everything, why wouldn't he talk?

3. My Last Try

"How about a day at the beach?" Dad asked the next Saturday.

Typical, I thought. This was the summer we were supposed to go camping in the redwoods up north. Instead, we could only make it as far as the beach, half an hour away. Still, anything was better than hanging around the house on such a hot day, so of course I said, "Yeah, let's go!" along with everyone else.

At first, Mama wanted to stay home with Clara, but Dad said it was time we had a family outing.

"We'll help with the baby," Shirley said, batting her long eyelashes. "Right, Rosie?"

Creep. I didn't answer. If Mama asked me to help, that was one thing, but Shirley could forget it if she thought I was going to take orders from her all day.

Our station wagon looked as if we were going away for the whole summer. (I wish.) We had a watermelon, folding chairs, an umbrella, two bags of baby stuff, suits and towels, and a picnic lunch. Dad tied our Boogy Boards and Clara's little porta-crib on top. Clara screamed the instant she was strapped into her car seat. Just when we were ready to leave, Katie yelled, "I need my straw hat." She ran inside to get it. Then Shirley went back for her "special" sun screen, and Mama decided she hadn't brought enough diapers. Finally, when we all had our belts on, the car started down the canyon, squealing like a pig every time it came to a stop sign.

After about ten minutes Katie called, "Mama, Silas has to go to the bathroom."

Mama groaned and looked in the rearview mirror. "Are you sure?"

"Make Silas ask," I muttered, but Dad gave me one of his warning looks.

"He has to go," Katie called.

So Mama pulled up at the next gas station, and we all waited while Dad took him into the bathroom. I leaned toward the front seat. "Mama, Katie always talks for Silas," I complained.

"I know," she said, sighing.

"What if he never learns to say anything?" Shirley asked. For once, it seemed, she was on my side.

When Mama didn't answer, I muttered, "He'll always be Silent Silas, that's all."

*   *   *

The beach was really crowded, and it took forever to unload our stuff, even with all of us carrying baskets and towels and coolers. I lugged the watermelon, which weighed a ton, and nearly dropped it in the sand. We walked a long time until we found an empty spot for the umbrella and Clara's porta-crib. I set the watermelon in the tiny spot of shade and did three cartwheels right into the water, landing upside down in the waves. As soon as I felt the cool water swirl around me, I forgot about my crazy family.

First Dan and I rode our Boogy Boards on top of the waves and got thrown off into the surf. We all built a giant sand castle with Dad; even Shirley helped without complaining that she was getting sandy. A little red-headed kid from up the beach joined in and started chattering with Katie and Silas like he'd always known them. "Silas doesn't talk," I warned him, but the red-headed boy looked at me like he couldn't care less and then went back to loading sand in Silas's bucket.

"Come on, Rosie, let's take a walk," Mama said. We went down the beach, and the most exciting thing happened—we saw six porpoises swimming right off-shore!

"Mama, look!" I yelled. "Let's follow them!"

Mama was already running near the water. I chased after her. The porpoises were swimming as fast as we could jog. They jumped out of the water, rolled over, and waved their fins. A few surfers tried to swim out to them, but the porpoises always stayed where no one could reach them. Once we even heard them squeak. When we got to the pier, they turned and went farther out to sea. I stood and watched them for a long, long time.

"Don't you love them?" I asked Mama.

She nodded. She was looking far away.

"When I grow up, I'm going to study whales and dolphins," I said, "after I'm done being a gymnast." I watched Mama. I'd never told her those secrets before.

"Wonderful," she said. "You can write a book about whales, and I'll illustrate it for you." She smiled at me. "Once you decide to do something, Rosie Maxwell, I've noticed that you usually get it done." She squeezed my hand.

"Even teaching Silas to talk?" I asked.

Mama frowned and shook her head. "That's something Silas has to do for himself, isn't it?" She sounded sad, like she was worried about him. "We'd better go back," she said. "Clara will be hungry."

Dumb me. Finally, I had two seconds alone with Mama and I had to spoil it by making her remember my stupid brothers and sisters. Even though she held my hand all the way back to our umbrella, I could tell she was thinking about something else.

Right away, everyone needed Mama. Clara wanted to be nursed, Dan had a cut on his knee, and Shirley whined, "I'm getting a sunburn right through my shirt." (Now that she had bumps on her chest, Shirley wore a T-shirt *over* her bathing suit. Why bother? After all, you could still see the bumps when the shirt was wet.)

Mama sat under the umbrella and pulled down the right side of her bathing suit to nurse Clara. "Mama!" Shirley screeched. She jumped in front of Mama, trying to hide her. "Do you have to do that when so many people are watching?"

"Who's watching?" Dad asked.

"It's perfectly natural," Mama said, giving Clara this peaceful, private look. Clara's tiny mouth gripped Mama's breast. All of a sudden, I felt like throwing sand at everyone.

"Let's give them some peace," Dad said. "Who wants an ice cream cone?"

We walked down the beach to a snack bar. A girl in a pink uniform wrote down our orders. "That's everyone but you, little boy," she said, leaning over the counter and smiling at Silas. "What would you like?"

"Make him say it," I hissed at Dad, but Katie piped up from under her straw hat, "He wants a chocolate cone with colored sprinkles on top."

"How do you know?" I demanded.

"I just do," Katie said.

That was the last straw. I decided I was going to make Silas talk today, no matter what. I thought about

it all afternoon until I'd figured out the one thing that
would probably do the trick.

I waited until we were almost ready to leave. Dad
had already taken two loads of stuff to the car. Shirley
was at the water fountain. Mama was jouncing Clara,
who was fussing and crying. Dan was in the car; Silas
was digging in the sand up near the parking lot. And
Katie was just where I wanted her—down the beach
with the red-headed boy.

"Rosie," Mama called to me as she picked up
Clara's bags, "get the twins and come along, will
you?"

This was it. When Mama was out of sight, I ran to
Katie. "Hide here a minute," I told her. "I want to
play a game with Silas."

"Why?" Katie looked suspicious. "What are you
going to do with him?"

"Um—nothing," I said. "Just play hide and seek.
You hide here, and I'll see if Silas can find you.
Okay?"

The red-headed boy looked up. His face was covered with freckles. "There's no place to hide at the
beach," he said.

"Sure there is," I said. "You can bury her."

Katie grinned and hugged herself. "Goody," she
said. She lay down on a towel. The red-headed boy
took his shovel and started covering her legs with sand.

"Stay here," I said to Katie, "we'll be right back."

I turned around to look for Silas, but he was gone. I ran up the beach. His little tracks went toward the parking lot.

All the way to the car, I could hear Clara bawling, Dad yelling, and Dan whining. "Hurry up!" Dad called to me. The engine was running, and Dad started to pull out as soon as I got in.

"Dad, wait," I said, but he was arguing with Mama.

"We would leave when it's too late to get out of here," he complained.

"Dad—" I whispered, but Shirley whirled around and gave me this cold look that said: Don't you know when to shut up?

"You're the one who wanted to stay all afternoon," Mama snapped at Dad, pulling up her shirt to feed Clara. (Didn't that kid ever stop eating?) Dan draped a towel over his head; he always hides when our parents argue. Shirley fiddled with the radio knobs in the front seat. I looked back toward the beach. Far away, I could see the flash of red hair and Katie's hat. We couldn't just *leave* her there, could we? Maybe Silas would pipe up before we left the parking lot. I turned around. Silas was sitting in back of me. His eyes were big and round and wet. "Say something," I whispered.

Clara stopped nursing and started to howl.

"Mama," Dan whined, "why can't I ever sit in front?"

"Because you're not old enough," Shirley said in her I'm-the-oldest voice.

"Dad!" I said. *"Dad—"*

The tape player blared a song by this disgusting heavy-metal group that Shirley likes. Dad snapped it off, grabbed the steering wheel, and rammed on the accelerator, shooting out into the traffic. "If—I—hear—one—more—sound," he said very loudly, *"I am going to lose my temper! Understand?"*

"But Dad—"

"No buts! The next person to speak is grounded for a week."

I clamped my mouth shut. I wasn't taking any chances. Trapped at home for a week with my family? I couldn't think of anything worse.

Yes I could. I craned my head toward the beach, but I couldn't see Katie anymore. What if we lost her?

4. Silas Leigh Maxwell

I refused to give up. As we inched down the highway toward the traffic light, I turned around and pleaded silently with Silas. *Now,* I thought, giving him this beady look. *Please,* Silas, I begged inside my head, *say* something. His face was as red as Shirley's sunburn, but he kept his lips clamped shut.

The light turned yellow before we got to the intersection. My dad put on the brakes and said a bad word. And then, from far in back, came a hiccup, then a small, scratchy voice I'd never heard before.

"Dad," it said very slowly, "Dad. Katie's . . . at . . . the . . . beach."

"Whooee!" I shouted, "Silas talked!"

But no one heard me because Mama was screaming bloody murder. "What!" she yelled. "Katie?" Her head swiveled around like a bird. "One, two, three, four, five—" she counted. "Oh, no!" she screamed.

She stared at Silas, alone in the jump seat. Tears ran down his cheeks. "God help us," Mama breathed, "my baby. Turn around, quick! Hurry!"

Dad swore and made a U-turn right in the middle of the traffic. Cars screeched and blew their horns. "It's okay," I yelled, "she's all right!" But my parents couldn't hear me, they were screaming so loud, and Clara was bawling at the top of her lungs.

"Rosie!" my dad yelled. "Why didn't you tell me before?"

"Dad—Silas is the one who—"

But Dad wasn't listening. He drove as if he were playing bumper cars, swerving all over the road and talking nonstop. He wheeled into the parking lot, and we all jumped out. "Shirley, take the baby," Mama said, shoving Clara into my sister's arms. "Silas, go with Dan. Rosie, you run with me."

"I'll find the lifeguard!" Dad shouted.

"Mama! Dad!" I yelled. "Wait!" They kept running, but Mama couldn't go very fast because her flip-flops kept slipping in the sand. I yanked on her cover-up. "Mama, stop!" I cried.

She almost fell over backward. "Rosie, let go!"

"Mama, Silas talked!" I said. "And I know where Katie is."

"Silas . . . what?" She whirled around and stared at me. Her eyes were all runny and red. "What did you say?"

"This isn't a time to make jokes," Shirley said, but I ignored her.

"Silas talked in the car," I said. "Didn't you hear him? He told you Katie was at the beach."

Mama stared at Silas. His face was all puffy and his thin hair was stuck to his forehead. "Is that right?" she asked.

Silas nodded. "Yes," he said. Mama gasped.

"Silas," I said softly. "You know where Katie is, don't you?"

He pointed his pudgy finger at me. "*You* left her."

Mama gave me this look that made me wish I were invisible. "Rosie Maxwell, if that's true—"

"Hurry up!" Dad yelled from down the beach. "What's wrong?"

We didn't answer him. "Silas can talk! Silas can talk!" Dan cried, hitting Silas on the back.

"Silas, say 'Shirley!' " my sister wheedled.

"Stop it," Mama snapped. "Take me to Katie this instant. Silas, where is she?"

Silas peered up the beach. "With the red boy," he said and took off.

"The red boy?" Dan asked, but Silas was already way ahead of us, his sturdy legs churning the sand. We followed him past our castle and up to the empty part of the beach. The red-headed boy was burying something next to Katie's straw hat.

Silas stopped and planted his feet. We stood back,

waiting to see what he'd do. Silas put his hands on his hips, stared at the boy, opened his mouth, and then closed it. Finally, he said in a scratchy voice, "Where's Katie?"

"Silas!" Dad gasped, but Mama shushed him. The hump in the sand moved. First two hands and feet burst out and then Katie's head popped up from under the sun hat. "Silas!" Katie cried. "You found me! Why did you take so long?"

Katie and Silas hugged each other. "Silas can talk!" Dan crowed. He wiggled his ears and crossed his eyes. "Silas, talk to me!" he sputtered.

Silas laughed. The tips of his ears were bright pink. "You're crazy," he whispered.

My dad hoisted Silas up in the air. "You rascal," he cried. "You had us fooled, all this time."

Silas frowned. "Put. Me. Down." He said each word slowly, like he was practicing.

"Can you say big words?" Shirley asked.

Silas made his lips into the shape of an O. "Po-po-cat-e-petyl," he said.

Shirley laughed. "That's a volcano!" she yelled. "Silas, you're a genius!"

"No I'm not." Silas's voice was hoarse, as if he had a cold. His smile went all the way across his face.

I stared at Silas. "I don't get it. How come you never said anything before?"

Silas smiled at Katie. They were holding hands. "I didn't need to," he said.

Even Dad's mouth dropped open. No one knew what to say.

Katie frowned at me. She was covered with sand, like salt stuck to a pretzel. "Why did you leave me so long?" Her lip trembled.

"So Silas would talk," I explained. Didn't anyone understand?

"Rosie," Mama said, in a very soft but *very* angry voice, "didn't you hear me tell you to bring the twins to the car?"

"It was only a game!" I cried. "I was going to tell you when we got to the stop light. I wanted Silas to talk, so you wouldn't worry about him anymore."

"Well, you gave us enough worry to last a lifetime," my dad said, wiping his eyes. "Katie could have drowned or wandered off. That was a very foolish thing to do."

Shirley jiggled Clara and gave me a dirty look. "I'll bet you never thought about all the things that could have happened."

"But you didn't even notice Katie was missing!" I yelled. "None of you did!"

Dad rubbed his beard. He looked embarrassed. "That has nothing to do with it." He gave Katie a hug. "We're just lucky we've got our girl back, that's all. Come on, twins, free rides for you both!" He picked them up, carrying one on each hip, and ran toward the car. Katie and Silas were squealing.

Mama took Clara and went ahead with Shirley. Even Dan gave me a sad look and hurried after Dad.

So who was the hero of the day? Not me, of course. I got Silas to talk, which is more than my parents, Dr. Crosby, or even Katie ever did. But did anyone say thanks? No. Not once. They just left me to walk alone to the car.

I tried doing a back flip, but instead I flopped sideways into the sand and twisted my arm. My hair was sticky with sand, but I didn't care. I stood up and brushed myself off, and that's when I noticed the bright yellow poster stapled onto a telephone pole.

"See the Cream of Young American Gymnasts," the sign read. "Come to the National Elite Gymnastics Meet. Saturday, September 21st. Watch Our Future Olympic Champions!"

There was a picture of a girl flying into a tuck over a balance beam. She looked about Shirley's age—well, maybe a little older.

I got goose bumps all over my legs. I was so excited, I did two cartwheels. My glasses fell off in the sand, and when I put them back on, I could hardly see, but I didn't care. I looked around quickly. No one was watching me. I tore the sign off the pole, stuffed it in my pocket, and ran to the car.

"Hurry up, Rosie!" my dad yelled.

"You're in the way back this time," Shirley said, looking down her nose at me.

I climbed into the jump seat next to Dan. He twisted around sideways and held his book up high in front of his face. Everyone ignored me, even Silas. You'd think maybe he'd thank me for breaking open his treasure box of words. But no, he just beamed and giggled while the family fussed over him, asking questions and cheering when he said stupid words like "caterpillar tractor," "bulldozer," and "Silas Leigh Maxwell," which is his whole name.

All that trouble for nothing. Silas wasn't anything like me, inside—or out. I watched the cars whizz past on the highway. Then, when I was sure Dan wasn't looking, I pulled the poster from my pocket and studied it again. The meet was at a high school in downtown Los Angeles. My parents would never take me there. I'd have to hitchhike or ride the bus. Fat chance.

I shook my head, scattering sand all over my legs, and crumpled the poster. I was doomed to spend the rest of my life trapped with my crazy family. But I'd show them. I'd practice until my hands were tough and calloused and my legs were all muscles. Someday, I'd be in a national meet. I'd vault higher than anyone else. I'd do a handstand pirouette on the parallel bars, and the judges would stand up and applaud. Then, maybe then, my family would notice me.

I sighed. *Maybe* they'd notice. That was the best I could hope for right now.

PART II
THE TROUBLE WITH AUGUST

1. The Surprise Visitor

For a while, summer seemed to go a little faster. I found another kid at day camp who liked doing gymnastics, and we learned some new tricks on the parallel bars. Shirley was having fun at art class, so she was off my case; Clara was waking up only once at night; and Mama and Dad were so happy Silas was talking that they forgot to be mad at me for leaving Katie.

I should have known things wouldn't be settled for long, though. I forgot about August 15. That's the day the twins have their birthday and the Maxwells get the "madhouse of the year" award.

In most families, kids play silly games like Pin the Tail on the Donkey when they have a birthday party. But this year, Mama told us a *real* donkey was coming to our house.

"*What?*" I shrieked. "Say what?"

Mama frowned. "Rosie Maxwell, I know you're not deaf. The Nelsons up in the canyon said we could

45

borrow their donkey for the party. He's very gentle.''
She smiled at me. "Chad Nelson offered to stay and
help give the kids rides, but I told him I was sure you
could handle Leroy yourself.''

I stared. "Leroy? That's the donkey's name?''
She nodded, smiling.
"Mama, I don't know a thing about donkeys.''
She shrugged. "There's nothing to it. You just walk
him up and down the road a few times.''
"You mean, lead him up the middle of the street?
What if a car comes?''
Mama laughed. "Dear heart, just tug him out of the
way. You'll be fine, I'm sure.''
Shirley was giggling, and I stuck out my tongue at
her. "Mama!" I protested. "Did you ever see the
Nelsons try to make that donkey go? He's the stubborn-
est animal I've ever seen!''
"Then I guess you'll be a fine match for each
other.''
"Mama! That's mean!''
Mama reached for my hand. "Calm down, Rosie,''
she said. "I'm sure you can manage. Please don't
shout. Now, Silas and Katie, let's discuss the rest of
the party.''
"Why can't Shirley do it?" I grumbled. Of
course, I knew the answer to that one. Shirley didn't
want to, so Shirley didn't have to. I stomped out of
the kitchen, insulted. How could my own mother
compare me to a donkey? I sat in the hall just outside

the kitchen door, close enough so I could still hear everything.

"You can each ask two friends," Mama was saying to Katie and Silas. "And we're going to have a special visitor that day."

"Who?" the twins asked. But Mama wouldn't tell them, no matter how much they begged and pleaded. And I certainly wasn't going to ask. If the visitor was anything like Leroy, the donkey, I wasn't interested.

Two days before the birthday, an old green pickup truck chugged along the street and parked in front of our house. We peered out the windows. "Grandma!" Dan and I shouted.

We scrambled over each other, raced outside and surrounded Grandma as she hopped from the cab. The twins wrapped their arms around her knees. Dan and Shirley took her hands, and I tickled my face with her long, gray braid. Grandma beamed and patted us, then kissed everybody. "Why, Rosie and Shirley, you look strong enough to come to the valley and work for me." Grandma's always promised that when we're older we can help out at her vegetable stand. She plunked right down on the grass so she was the same height as the twins. "How's the birthday pair?"

We held our breath. "We're fine, Grandma," Silas whispered.

Grandma crowed like a peacock and hugged Silas

until he squirmed. "Why, Silas honey, no one told me you could talk."

Shirley beamed. "We wanted to surprise you."

"Well, you certainly did." Grandma wiped her eyes and took Silas's hand, pulling herself back up. "Where's that baby sister of yours?"

We dragged Grandma inside. She hugged Mama and fussed over Clara. "Beautiful," she said, "she's just beautiful." Grandma beamed at Clara, then winked at me. "Rosie, I believe she looks like you."

I was so pleased, I hugged myself. I couldn't say a word.

Shirley nudged me. "Guess she means you and Clara have the same blotchy face."

Grandma laughed. "Just you wait. One day, Clara will be proud to resemble our Rose."

"Just pray she doesn't get Rosie's hair," Shirley muttered so only I could hear.

But I didn't care. If Grandma thought I was beautiful, that was enough for me. And to thank her, I lugged her duffel bag into the house all by myself. We also brought in a giant watermelon and some crates of fruit and vegetables from her farm. When everything was inside, Grandma, Shirley, and Mama sat together on the couch. They looked like sisters with their long braids, black eyes, and blue jeans. The rest of us squinched as close to Grandma as we could.

"I'm sorry I couldn't come sooner," Grandma told

Mama. "I just had too many crops to harvest." She smiled. "A lot's happened since the last time I came down. You had five kids, now there are six. That's a big change!"

"You're not kidding," I said, and even Mama laughed.

"I'm so glad I got here in time for the party," Grandma went on. "Silas and Katie, what do you want for your birthday?"

"A new pet." We stared at Silas. His voice still surprised us, it was so deep and husky.

Grandma just nodded, like she'd heard him talk for years. "That sounds like a good present," she said. "What kind?"

"Now wait a minute," Mama interrupted. "Silas, your lizard is still lost somewhere in the kitchen. I don't think we need any more animals. Besides, you can always go up to the Nelsons' if you want to pet some rabbits or feed the chickens."

Silas's eyes got big and wet. "I want my *own* animal," he said.

"Of course you do." Grandma pulled Silas onto her lap. Mama shook her head so hard I thought her earrings would fly off, but Grandma didn't seem to notice. "Kittens and puppies are too much work, when you have a baby. Is there any other kind of pet you'd like? Something small? How about some fish?" Grandma suggested.

Silas shook his head. "Not fish," he said. "I want a noo-sual pet."

"You mean, *un*usual?" Shirley corrected him.

Silas nodded.

"Oh great!" I said. "How about an iguana, Silas? Or an alligator? So cozy to sleep with at night."

Silas's lip trembled. "Alligators bite," he whispered.

"And iguanas growl," I said, making a deep growly noise in my throat.

"Rosie—" Mama warned.

Grandma hugged Silas. "I'll bet we can find you an unusual pet."

Silas gave her a sloppy kiss and slid off her lap, then Katie climbed on. They looked like kids in the mall, taking turns with Santa.

"What about you, Katie?" Grandma asked.

"I want a crawl doll," Katie said right away, like she'd planned it for months.

"A what?" we all asked.

"A crawl doll," Katie said. "I saw it in the toy store. It crawls and talks and cries and wets, just like a real baby."

"Geez, Katie, we've got one of those," I said, pointing at Clara. "She cries and wets all the time."

Katie crossed her arms over her chest and puffed out her cheeks. Her pigtails stuck out straight so she looked like Pippi Longstocking. "I want my *own* baby to take care of,'' she said. ''I want a crawl doll.''

''Hmmm—interesting that Silas and Katie both want something to cuddle,'' Grandma said, winking at Mama. ''I guess Rosie and I will have to go on a little expedition.''

2. Shopping with Grandma

The next day, Mama let me skip day camp so I could go to the toy store with Grandma. Shirley wanted to come too, but Mama told her she couldn't miss her last art class. So it was just Grandma and me poking along in her truck, talking loud over the hiss of the cars zooming past.

When we got off the freeway and pulled into the parking lot, we were hot and sticky. "One trouble with my old truck," Grandma said, "it's not air-conditioned."

"I like your truck," I said.

It was cool inside the store. We marched up and down the aisles, looking at a zillion toys, until we found the doll section. There were rubber baby dolls, stiff Barbie dolls, dolls dressed like ballet dancers, black dolls with soft curly hair. We found the crawl doll on the bottom shelf, in a big box with a plastic window. We stared at it for a few minutes. The crawl doll was almost as big as Katie. She had short plastic-looking fake hair. Her face was fat and wide, with no expression, and her pasty arms and legs looked as if someone had twisted them.

"What do you think?" Grandma asked.

"It's the ugliest doll I've ever seen," I said.

Grandma chuckled. "I agree. I never did care much for dolls," she added.

"Me neither." We grinned like we'd just discovered the best secret about each other.

"Well," Grandma said at last. "This is what Katie wants. And it's not too expensive. I guess we're stuck."

I picked out a bright yellow hard hat for Silas to wear when he pretended to be a bulldozer operator. I didn't know what to get for Katie, so I looked around while Grandma bought something for Clara. Right in front of me was a rack full of baby bottles. I picked one up and pinched its pudgy nipple. It felt rubbery and soft between my fingers.

"Can I help you, little girl?"

I turned around and glared at the saleslady. "I'm buying this for my baby sister," I said and stomped over to Grandma. I hate it when grown-ups call me "little girl." Thank goodness, Shirley wasn't around.

"Gracious, Rosie, your cheeks are the color of a ripe tomato." Grandma laughed. "What's wrong?"

"Nothing," I muttered, handing her the bottle. "I'm giving this to Katie—for her new doll."

"Good idea," Grandma said.

We went to the checkout counter. Grandma bought batteries for the crawl doll and stuck them in her bag. Our arms were full. Grandma put the doll behind her seat in the cab. "Now you'll have two screaming babies in the house," she chuckled.

Grandma obviously thought that was funny. But I didn't.

"What about Silas's present?" I asked, as we drove down a busy street. "Are you really buying him a pet?"

"I'm not sure," Grandma said. "We'll see what they have. It needs to be something that lives outside and isn't much trouble."

"I wonder why he wants something unusual?" I asked.

"Silas is a little unusual himself, don't you think?" Grandma said, smiling.

I laughed. "You can say that again." It was cozy talking to Grandma; she seemed to understand everything. "Let's get him an anteater," I giggled, thinking about the rain forest book Mama was illustrating. "Or a tapir." Mama's tapir looked like a hippo, a pig, and an ugly dog mixed up together.

"We'll just have to see." Grandma turned onto another busy street, drove over to the curb, and studied her map book. "Almost there," she said. After about four traffic lights, she pulled up in front of a tiny store. "Venice Pets," the sign read. Underneath, in small letters, it said, "Strange and Exotic Animals."

"Ex-o-tic—" I read. "What's that?"

"It's just a fancy way of saying the animals are unusual," Grandma answered. "Just what Silas wants."

We got out of the truck and stood in front of the window. Some funny puppies were playing in a basket; they had so much fur on their faces you couldn't see their eyes. A huge parrot with an orange beak was swinging on a bar above the puppies.

"Now there's an exotic pet," Grandma said, pointing at a big washtub.

I stared. A gigantic, I mean really humongous, snake was sleeping in the tub. Its body was thicker than my leg, and it was coiled up so many times, it filled the washtub to the brim, like some kind of weird laundry.

I grabbed Grandma's sleeve. "You're not buying him *that*, are you?"

"Don't worry; I'm not interested in pythons. Come on, let's go inside."

I wasn't so sure, until Grandma said, "Look—there's glass on the other side of the snake, too. He can't get out."

So I followed her into the store, keeping an eye on the python. Luckily, he didn't budge.

It was noisy in that shop. Birds chirped and twittered, Siamese kittens yowled, and a fat puppy with a wrinkled face whimpered at us.

"Grandma, look," I said. "That puppy's like an old lady with lots of extra skin."

"May I help you?" asked the man behind the counter.

Grandma went to talk with him while I looked around. There was a monkey in a cage who looked frisky but sad. I thought about setting him free in our eucalyptus tree, but I knew Mama wouldn't allow it. There were some fluffy kittens in a box, but kittens weren't unusual. Beside them was a guinea pig that smelled like old sawdust and made a weird squeaking noise.

I went to the back of the store where it was dark except for some funny purple lights. A tiny skunk was huddled in a big cage. He watched me with shiny black eyes and held up a puffy tail that was almost as big as his body. Would he spray me? He was a little bit smelly.

"Grandma!" I called. "There's a baby skunk back here."

Grandma and the pet shop man came over. "These are our nocturnal animals," the man said, turning on a light. "I keep them in the dark during the day so they'll think it's night and be more active. The skunk's a cutie. Someone brought him in here when his mother was killed.''

The man unhooked the door of the cage and reached for the skunk, pulling him out. I held my nose and jumped backward, and the man laughed.

"Don't worry," he said, "he's de-skunked."

"What's that mean?" I asked.

The man smiled. "We removed his little sprayer, so he won't smell up your house."

Grandma sniffed suspiciously. "Is it really a house pet?" she asked.

"Skunks can live outside or in," the man answered. "Want to hold him?" he asked me.

I held out my hands, keeping them a long way from my body. The skunk's feet were prickly and sharp, but his fur was softer than a puppy's. His beady black eyes stared at me, and then he slowly raised his tail. Nothing smelly came out, but I gave him back to the man anyway. I wasn't taking any chances. Still, the skunk was cute. And he looked so lonesome in that wire cage, without even a cozy place to sleep.

"Let's get him," I said. "He won't be any trouble. And Silas wanted something different. A skunk sure is unusual."

"Well—" Grandma began.

"If he doesn't work out, you can always bring him back," the man said.

So we bought the skunk, a cage, a water bottle, and kitten chow, which is what the man said he liked to eat. Grandma tied the cage into the back of the truck so it wouldn't slide around while we were driving. When she got into the cab, she leaned against the seat and laughed so hard she had to wipe her eyes.

"A skunk, and an ugly doll that cries," she gasped. "This may be the last time your parents invite *me* for a visit!"

Grandma kept the skunk hidden in the back of her truck overnight. The twins were so excited about decorating their cake with tons of colored sprinkles that they never noticed Grandma tiptoe outside with a dish of milk and little bits of kitty food hidden in a paper bag. Dan stayed late at a friend's house, and Shirley was on the phone for hours, yammering with her girlfriends about some boy.

But Mama was curious. "What *did* you buy?" she whispered after supper. "You both look like the cat that swallowed the canary."

Grandma just shrugged and winked at me. "Well, we didn't buy a canary—or a cat. Rosie picked out something very original," she said.

Mama threw up her hands. "It better be something easy to manage, that's all I can say."

3. Four Plus Four Makes Trouble

The next morning, Silas and Katie ran into the room I share with Shirley and pounced on us, yelling, "We're eight years old! We're eight years old!"

Shirley groaned and pulled the sheet over her head.

"Huh?" I said, rubbing my eyes. "Since when?"

"I'm four, and Silas is four," Katie said, bouncing up and down on my knees. "Four plus four makes eight, right?"

"Four plus four makes trouble," I said, but I hugged them anyway. Their faces were smiley and bright. "Happy birthday, guys."

We had French toast with mango slices for breakfast, and then we went into the living room to let the twins open their presents. There were so many packages, it seemed like Christmas had come but Santa had forgotten Dan, Shirley, Clara, and me.

Mama and Dad gave Katie an easel they had made, with a new set of paints and a smock with stenciled animals. They gave Silas a power shovel big enough for him to sit on; the crane was as tall as he was and the levers really worked.

"Wow!" Silas said. He opened up his new hard hat, grinned, and put it right on his head. He sat down on the shovel and tried to pick up wrapping paper with the scoop, making growling and clanking noises.

"Where are *your* presents, Grandma?" Katie asked.

"Katie," Shirley said, "that's rude."

But Grandma didn't think so. She pulled the big package from behind the couch and we all waited while Katie tore the paper off the box. "Here she is!" Katie squealed, holding up the doll. Its arms and legs were still stuck in this weird position, like a baby playing freeze tag. "How does it crawl?" Katie asked, shaking her.

Grandma gave me the batteries, and I put them in the little hatch in the doll's back, then showed Katie how to turn the doll on.

Katie's chubby fingers twisted the switch. The crawl doll began to move. Her head turned slowly from side to side, like some old lumbering cow, then her arms and legs twitched, and pretty soon she was creeping across the rug. Suddenly, her mouth dropped open and she made a terrible, screeching, squawking sound. I thought all the neighborhood tomcats were fighting in our living room.

"Ouch!" Mama cried, covering her ears.

"Holy Toledo!" Dad groaned.

"My goodness!" Grandma gasped.

Clara started to scream as loud as the doll. We all covered our ears and stood in a circle, staring at the crawl doll as if it came from another planet. It made a gurgly, babbly noise, rammed into Dad's shins, and then squealed like someone being choked.

"Turn that thing off!" my dad roared.

Katie picked the doll up, hugged her tight, and said, "It's okay, Mirna—don't cry." She turned the switch and the doll stopped howling. Its head was twisted to the side and its eyes were half open.

"Mirna?" my dad asked, raising his eyebrows at Grandma.

"Grandma gave me the doll, so I'm naming it after her," Katie said.

For some reason, Dad thought that was really funny, but Grandma pursed her lips tight and just said, "Well, Silas—your turn. Let's go outside."

We followed Silas and Grandma out to the big eucalyptus tree in the front yard. Grandma's tarp was still covering the cage. "Silas, sit down and close your eyes," Grandma said. "No one else should look either, except Rosie."

Grandma beckoned for me to help her take the cover off the cage. I unhooked the latch. The skunk was hiding in the far corner, blinking its eyes in the bright light. Shirley sniffed. "Something smells gross," she complained.

Grandma chuckled and set the skunk in Silas's lap. He opened his eyes, stared, and then laughed out loud. "A skunk!" he yelled, stroking its fur.

"How disgusting." Shirley glared at me. "I bet this was your idea."

"I think he's cute," Dan said. I smiled at him. Good old Dan. He was almost always on my side— which was more than I could say for the rest of the people in my house.

Mama and Dad looked at each other and then stared at Grandma. "Mom, I don't know—" Mama began.

"He's deskunked," I said quickly. "He won't smell."

Dad wrinkled his nose. "What's the odor drifting around right now—perfume?"

"The pet store man said we could bring him back if we didn't like him," I said.

"Rufus isn't going back," Silas said.

"Rufus?" my dad said. "How do you kids name everything so fast?"

The skunk's nose was twitching like a rabbit. "Here, Rufus," Katie said, kneeling down. "Mirna wants to say hi." She turned the doll on.

"Don't!" Dan yelled, but it was too late. Mirna squawked, the skunk raised its tail, and this time there really *was* a skunk smell. Even though it wasn't very strong, we all held our noses.

"Deskunked, eh?" Dad asked, glaring at Grandma.

"He is," Grandma said. She turned the switch on the crawl doll's back. "Let's keep Mirna and Rufus apart until Rufus gets used to things here."

"*I* may never get used to Rufus—*or* Mirna," Mama muttered.

4. Leroy Joins the Party

After lunch, the other kids arrived, and everyone wanted to play with Mirna and Rufus. Each time the crawl doll screamed, the kids yelled too. Then they'd watch the skunk until it lifted its tail, which made them screech and run all over the yard. Pretty soon Clara was bawling at the top of her lungs, and in the middle of the racket, we heard a loud *"Hee-haw!"* from the road.

"Leroy's here!" Silas cried and ran toward the street with all the kids behind him. Dad grabbed the doll and shut her off. Clara's face was almost purple.

"I'm going to the garage for earplugs!" Dad complained.

"I should think you'd be used to this kind of racket after listening to your band play!" Mama called after him. She was bouncing Clara, and her face was squinched up the way it gets when she has a headache.

"My band has *never* been as bad as this!" Dad shouted back as he went outside.

64

I looked at Grandma. "I think we made a big mistake. *Two* big mistakes."

Grandma's eyes twinkled. "They'll get over it," she whispered. "But maybe we'd better go outside and see what's happening in the yard."

The Nelsons were waiting on the grass, smiling, with the donkey right behind them. Mr. and Mrs. Nelson both had gray ponytails all the way down their backs, and they always wore faded jeans and tie-dyed shirts. Their beat-up van was covered with "Grateful Dead" stickers.

"Leroy's ready," Chad Nelson said. He handed me the rope attached to the donkey's halter. "Your mom said you'd be in charge."

"Hi, Leroy." The donkey's ears flicked forward when I talked. I hated to admit it, but Leroy was sort of cute. He had long eyelashes, like Katie's, and bristly fur. When I stuck out my hand, he nuzzled it with his soft nose.

Grandma started some games with the other kids while I gave donkey rides. Maureen, one of Katie's friends, got on first. Leroy trotted a few feet up the street, then planted his hooves and wouldn't budge. I dragged on the rope, then pushed Leroy's behind. He still wouldn't go.

"Come on, Leroy," I grunted, shoving. He refused to move until he spotted something up the street and broke into a trot. He was headed right for Mrs. Stone's flower bed, filled with yellow and orange marigolds. I ran beside him to keep up, holding Maureen's knee so she wouldn't fall off. "Ooo!" Maureen yelled.

When we got to the flower bed, Leroy stopped and nibbled the marigolds. "Leroy, no!" I said, jerking the rope. He kept right on munching. I looked around. No sign of Mrs. Stone. I plucked a flower, waggled it under Leroy's nose, and whispered, "Come on, boy, get the flower." He sniffed, and reached with his teeth. I backed away, and Leroy followed me.

That's how I kept him moving for three more rides. I picked a flower at Mrs. Stone's, ran back to our yard, held it under his nose, and walked backward up the hill. When the kids were ready to turn around, I let Leroy eat the flower, then ran him back to the house. I felt like a real idiot, but luckily, there wasn't a whole lot of traffic on the street that day.

Only two more rides, I thought, when Silas and Katie came out to the street.

"We want to go together," Katie said, clutching her doll. Silas had his hands folded over his stomach. He looked sort of fat, and he smelled skunky.

"No dolls on this donkey ride," I said. "Where's Rufus?"

"Asleep," Silas said.

"Please can Mirna come?" Katie begged. "She'll be quiet."

"Okay, okay," I said. Anything to get this over with fast.

I helped Katie on first, and Silas climbed up behind

her. Leroy started to prance. He turned his head, stretched his nose back to sniff Silas's leg, and shied sideways.

"Whoa, Leroy!" I yelled, hanging onto the rope. Just then, Rufus's head poked out from under Silas's T-shirt, and Leroy really spooked. The doll fell off, howling. *"Hee-haw!"* Leroy squealed. He bucked, then took off up the street with his rope dangling, leaving me lying in the road. Silas and Katie clutched his fur, screaming "Whoa, Leroy!"

Leroy galloped to the flower bed and screeched to a stop like someone stomping on the brakes in a fast car. The twins tumbled into the grass, and Mrs. Stone came running down her walk, waving a shovel.

"Oh no," I groaned, scrambling to my feet. When I got to Mrs. Stone's yard, Katie was sobbing, Silas was crawling through the flowers, making little clucking noises and calling, "Here Rufus!" while Leroy chomped on flowers like Ferdinand the bull.

"What on earth is going on here?" Mrs. Stone shrieked. "Get this pony out of my yard."

I ran up, totally out of breath. "It's a donkey," I gasped, trying to comfort Katie. Mrs. Stone's face was as purple as the tall flowers beside her.

"I don't care if he's an elephant, get him out of my flower bed!" Mrs. Stone yelled. When Leroy started nibbling a pink rose bush, Mrs. Stone slapped his rump with her shovel.

"Don't, you'll hurt him!" I shouted. "Anyway, it

was just an accident—you don't have to get so mad.''

''Watch your manners, young lady,'' Mrs. Stone snapped.

''Here, Rufus,'' Silas whispered, clicking his fingers. Mrs. Stone bent over to stare at him. ''What is that child doing—eeek!'' Mrs. Stone dropped the shovel and sank down in her flowers, groaning, as the skunk ran across her feet and skittered under a hedge with Silas right behind him. Leroy moved on to the next rosebush. I couldn't help it—I had to laugh, even though Mrs. Stone was so mad, she looked like a bottle of soda that was shaken up so much it was about to fizz over.

Just then, my dad came tearing up the street. ''What's going on?'' he puffed.

We all stared at him for a second.

''It wasn't my fault—'' I began.

''I lost Mirna,'' Katie sobbed.

''Rufus ran away, but I caught him!'' Silas announced, running up to us. The skunk was tucked under his arm with his tail flying out like a little black and white flag. When Mrs. Stone saw Rufus, she opened her mouth, pointed, and let her chin waggle. No sounds came out. Finally she gasped, ''Get all these *creatures* out of here!''

Silas whirled around and ran down the street, clutching Rufus. Dad apologized to Mrs. Stone, helped her up, and said we'd be back to fix her flower bed after the party. We dragged Leroy out to the road, and then Dad picked up Katie and set her on his shoulder.

"Mirna!" Katie screeched. "We left Mirna!"

Good grief. Wasn't this terrible day ever going to be over? I ran down the street, found Mirna, and dusted her off. Then I dashed back to Leroy. "Come on, you stupid donkey," I said. "You started this."

My dad looked at me over his shoulder. "Katie and Silas had no business riding that donkey together or bringing that wretched doll. And as for the skunk—"

"Dad!" I protested, "How was I supposed to know Silas had the skunk under his shirt?"

"If you and your grandmother had any sense, you wouldn't have bought that noisy doll *or* that stinking animal in the first place. I've got a good mind to return them both," he snapped.

"No!" Katie sobbed, "you can't take Mirna back!"

"How come you don't return Clara to the store?" I asked Dad's back. "She yells too, and she stinks even worse than Rufus, if you ask me."

"I *didn't* ask you," Dad said, and kept on walking.

5. Clara's Smile

I took Leroy into our yard, tied him to a tree, and gave him an old bucket with some water in it. Silas settled Rufus in his cage, making him a little bed of grass. The other kids stood around, looking worried, while Katie choked. "I w-w-want Mir-rna."

"Take your stupid doll," I said, handing it to her. "She's nothing but trouble."

"Now, now." Grandma carried Katie inside, wiped her face and put a Band-Aid on her elbow where it was scraped. I stretched out my legs, hoping Grandma would notice my bloody knees, but she was too busy with Katie.

"Let's give Mirna a nap," Grandma said. Katie sniffled as she put Mirna in Clara's cradle and covered her with a blanket.

"Hey, Katie," I said, trying to cheer her up. I mean, it *was* her birthday, after all. "You forgot to open your present from me." I gave her the little package, with a card I'd spent about an hour making. I'd even drawn a picture of a unicorn, Katie's favorite animal, but she didn't notice. She tore off the wrapping paper and gave me a nasty look.

"I don't need a bottle," she said in a cross voice. "I'm four years old."

"It's not for you, dummy," I said. "It's for your baby."

"I'm not a dummy!" Katie screamed, and she threw the bottle at me. "Mama, Rosie called me a dummy. I hate you!"

Oh, boy, I thought, this is what I get for being nice to my sister?

Mama came out of the kitchen with a stack of paper cups and a jug of juice. Shirley whisked through, carrying the cake. She didn't even look at me.

"Calm down, everyone," Mama said, even though her voice wasn't calm at all. "Katie, bring your friends to the picnic table for dessert."

Katie gulped, wiped her eyes and ran outside. "Silas! Our cake is ready!" she yelled.

Mama and Grandma went out after her. The door slammed, and then the living room was so quiet I took a lot of deep breaths and listened to them fill my stomach. I tiptoed to the cradle and pulled the blanket off the crawl doll. "Crybaby," I said, turning her on. She twisted her neck, opened her mouth, and screeched. I picked her up and held her, but she was hard and bony, not warm and wet like Clara. "Quiet!" I said, turning her off. She closed her mouth, and the crying stopped.

"Magic, isn't it?"

I whirled around. Dad was in the doorway, swaying from side to side, holding Clara. His bald spot was all sweaty, and his glasses were sliding off the end of his nose. "If only we could turn Clara off as easily as that monster," he said.

I scowled. Even though it was nice to know Dad felt the same way about Clara's crying, I was still mad at him.

"Sorry I was so cross," Dad said. "It wasn't fair to blame Leroy's bad behavior on you."

"Leroy's okay, actually," I admitted. "He spooked because of the skunk and the doll."

Dad laughed. "Can't say as I blame him." He put his hand on my shoulder. "You and your grandma were right. Silas and Katie both need something to cuddle now that Clara's born. It's just too bad Katie wanted something so *un*cuddly," Dad added. "And knowing Silas, he'll squeeze that skunk to death, smell or no smell."

"I don't know how to fix the skunk's smeller," I said, "but I can keep Mirna from making noise."

Dad grinned at me. "What did you have in mind?"

I opened the little hatch on the doll's back, turned the batteries around, and closed it up again.

"Clever," my dad said. "Who taught you how to do that?"

"You did," I said. "Remember when you changed the batteries on Dan's fire truck, the one that squirted water and made a real siren noise?"

"Oh, yeah. That was almost as bad as Mirna, wasn't it?" Dad chuckled. "I don't think your grandmother likes having the crawl doll named for her." He looked at Clara. Her eyelids fluttered. Dad hummed a little tune and kept on swaying until Clara was all the way asleep. He frowned at the plastic lump in the cradle. "We can't put her in with Mirna, can we? And the kids might wake her up if she's in our bedroom. They're playing right under our windows."

"She can sleep in my room," I said. So we went upstairs, made a little pad for Clara on the rug between the beds, and covered her with a sweater.

"Whew!" my dad said when we were out in the hall. "I thought she'd never stop." He tweaked my hair. "Can you keep an ear out for the *real* baby? I want to help your mom with the cake."

"Sure," I said. "But I have to get something first."

We went downstairs. When Dad was outside, I filled the baby bottle with apple juice and took it upstairs to my room. Clara was sound asleep. I closed the door and lay across my bed, looking out the window. It was like watching a mixed-up TV comedy with the sound turned off. Grandma was sitting cross-legged on the grass, telling a story to Katie and some of the kids. Shirley was lounging on the patio, twisting the long telephone cord that came out through the kitchen window as she talked to her friends. Across the yard, Leroy was eating the bark off the eucalyptus tree. Dan sat in the sandbox, reading a new book someone had brought the twins. Silas was trying to get the skunk to crawl into his hard hat.

But the weirdest thing was my parents: Mama was swinging from the rope swing that hangs from the big tree, and Dad was walking around the picnic table, eating leftover hunks of cake. They looked as though they'd forgotten how to be grown-ups.

I slipped off the bed and sat down next to Clara. Her tiny back went up and down underneath my sweater. "Poor kid," I said. "You *would* have to get born into this crazy family." I kissed her soft head and she made a tiny sighing noise. "Maybe you'll turn out normal," I whispered. "There's always a chance."

Then two things happened that were weird and special at the same time. Clara smiled at me, right there in her sleep! Instead of looking ugly and cross, her face was really cute—just for a second. Then her lips and cheeks went in and out, like she was nursing.

"You're okay, actually," I whispered. "Even if everyone pays attention to you instead of me." I put my head on the rug and studied Clara's face. "And Grandma says you'll grow up to be beautiful like me. Lucky you. We can be the four-eyed frizz twins."

I climbed up on my bed and took a sip of juice. It

tasted sweet, sucked through the rubber nipple. I lay back against the pillow and drank the whole thing, holding the bottle up like I was a baby again and some-one was cuddling *me*, for a change. Clara made a soft, cooing sound, and then we both slept for a long, long time.

PART III
SCHOOL BLUES

1. First Day of School

After the twins' birthday, no one wanted Grandma to leave. She stayed a few extra days, but then she had to go home to her farm. "I've got to catch up with my vegetables," she said.

We were all crabby when she left. Dad had school meetings, so Mama never got into her studio. Clara had a rash that made her cry. Even Silas and Katie, who never argue, fought over their new toys. Shirley was on my case every minute, and I never saw Dan; he went through at least four or five new library books every week.

So, for the first time in my whole life, I was actually excited when school started. For six hours every day, I could escape from my family. At least, that's what I thought.

By seven o'clock on the first morning, I'd already changed my shorts three times, stuck barrettes in my hair (what a joke), tried on sandals, then sneakers, then sandals again. That was nothing compared to Shirley. She wiggled into so many outfits there was a mountain of clothes on our floor.

"I look awful!" Shirley screeched, standing in front of the mirror for the millionth time. She was wearing a yellow skirt and a T-shirt with a surfer cresting a giant wave.

"No you don't," I said. For some reason, that seemed to make her happy, and she ran downstairs at last. As for me, I wouldn't dream of looking in the mirror, or if I did, I'd leave my glasses off. I'd rather see myself in a blur.

I went to the kitchen and was just poking my nose into the refrigerator, wondering what to make for lunch, when Mama decided to ruin my day before it had even started.

"Rosie," she said quietly, "I was hoping you'd get Dan settled in first grade this morning."

I turned around and stared at her. "That's *your* job," I said.

"Not really," Mama answered. "I have to take the twins to preschool, and Clara has a doctor's appointment. Your dad is giving Shirley a ride to junior high on his way to work. Besides, I'm sure Dan would rather have you take him than me. Right, Dan?"

Dan sat with his elbows on the table and a book in his lap, nibbling Cheerios. "Huh?" he asked.

"Well—" I began, but Mama was too quick for me.

"Thanks, Rosie." She gave me this big, cheerful smile. "It's nice to know I can count on you. Dan's in Mr. Cutting's class, and so is Andrew."

Andrew was Dan's best friend. They both stayed at the School in the Canyon for kindergarten last year, instead of coming to my school. "Why can't Dan go in with Andrew?" I asked.

"He can," Mama said, "but they need to know where their room is."

"I don't need help," Dan said suddenly, blinking at us. "I can read the signs. I'll find Mr. Cutting's room myself."

Mama winked at me. "Just check with the office," she said. "I called the school yesterday to tell them you'd be bringing him in. It will be as easy as pie."

I sighed. I had a funny feeling she might be wrong.

We left early because I knew Dan would stop and study every tiny caterpillar and rock. I tried to make him hurry down our dusty street. For a little while I felt grown up, showing him where to cross, how to sneak past the huge dog that always barks—all the things Shirley taught me when we used to walk to school together.

When we passed the School in the Canyon, Dan stopped and peered over the wooden fence. "Too bad we can't go here anymore," he said.

"We're too old," I said. I stood beside him and looked into the cozy playground. Rachel, the teacher, was putting trucks and buckets into the sandbox. I remembered when I was so short I couldn't see over the fence.

Rachel waved to us. "Hello, Rosie! Hi, Dan!" she called. "Good luck in school!"

We waved back. It used to be so much fun to build houses with the big cardboard blocks. Rachel let us make messes with mud and dough, and there was never any homework. For a minute, I wished I were going there too. But then I wouldn't be with Leah, my best friend.

"Come on," I said to Dan. He came, but he kept looking over his shoulder all the way to the flashing light.

Things started out okay. We got to school early, so I had time to go inside and find out that Leah and I both had the new fourth-grade teacher, Ms. Pingree. I was nervous, of course—I mean, who wouldn't be, with a teacher named Ms. Pingree? What would she be like? Thank goodness, Leah was in my class; we could survive it together. Outside the office, Dan found Andrew and his mother, who said she'd take them both to their classroom. Thank goodness.

"Good luck!" I gave Dan a little pinch on the arm.

"See you after school, okay?" He gave me this casual wave, like he was already used to school, and went upstairs. I ran back outside; I could hear the big yellow buses roaring into the parking lot.

Leah was one of the first ones off, as usual. She liked to sit in front so she wouldn't get sick. I ran over and we grinned at each other.

"Hey," she said.

"Hey," I said back. Her hair was all done up in corn rows, and she had on a bright pink skirt. She looked fancy compared to me, and for a second I felt shy. But then she grabbed my hand and dragged me to our special corner.

"Long time," she said. Leah lives so far away, we don't see each other much in the summer. She rides to our school on the freeway with lots of other kids who live near downtown Los Angeles. Luckily, our moms don't mind if we talk on the phone, so Leah knew about Clara.

"How's the baby?" she asked. "She ever stop bawling?"

"Sometimes," I said. "Actually, she's sort of cute. She looks like Katie. She gets all the attention, though."

"Of course," Leah said. "Babies always do. Just like new stepkids."

"You mean Robert?" I asked. We jumped on the hopscotch board while we talked. Robert was

Leah's new stepbrother. He was six years old, like Dan.

"Yeah," Leah said. "Now my mom has a different job, so after school, I have to help Gran look after Cary *and* Robert, who's a pain in the you-know-what."

"What does he do?" I asked.

"Oh, you know—the usual stuff. He's just a brat," she said. "Whatever he wants, he gets."

"Yeah," I said. "Little kids are like that. And whatever they decide to do, they do."

If only I hadn't said that.

When the ball rang, I was so busy saying hi to everybody in the halls that I almost missed Dan. He was leaning against the wall outside our classroom, and his face was bright pink under his freckles.

"What are you doing here?" I said. "Do you want to get in trouble before school even starts?"

He crossed his arms. "This school stinks," he said. "They don't do anything right."

"What do you mean?" I asked.

He shrugged. "I'm in the wrong class."

I looked at Leah. She raised her eyebrows. "Didn't you find Mr. Cutting's room?" I asked.

"Of course," Dan said. "But I shouldn't be there."

Dan sounded like one of the characters in the books he reads. As far as I could see, he was making no sense. "So where do you want to go?" I asked him him. "Back to the School in the Canyon?"

Dan gave me a funny look. "Maybe I'll do that," he said, starting down the hall.

"Come on," I said, grabbing his arm, "don't be silly. You have to stay in first grade when you're six. It's a law. Right, Leah?"

"Right," she said, but Dan shook his head, twisting away from me as if I had cooties.

"I don't have to if I don't want to," he said.

"Yes, you do," I said. "Want Leah and me to walk you upstairs?"

Dan shoved his hands into his pockets. For a second, he looked like a tiny copy of our dad. "I can go myself," he said and stomped off down the hall, tripping over his shoelaces. He was so small compared to all the big kids that I felt bad, watching him tromp along by himself.

"Think he'll be okay?" I asked Leah.

"Probably. I wonder what's eating him?" she said.

"Who knows. Maybe some kid looked at him cross-eyed or something. Everyone hates first grade, don't they?"

Before Leah could answer, we heard heels clicking along the hall. A short woman was rushing toward us holding a microscope under one arm and a couple of big animal bones under the other. She had a wide, crooked smile.

"Good morning, girls," she said to us. "All ready for fourth grade?"

Was this our teacher? And why was she carrying bones and a microscope? Leah and I grinned at each other and followed her into the room. Maybe school would be fun this year.

2. Allergic to My Family

The first thing I noticed about Ms. Pingree was her feet: she had on bright green cowboy boots with squiggly designs. Her hair was cut almost as short as Dan's, and she had a funny, drawly way of talking. I decided that I might like her because she let Leah and me sit together. After everyone was settled and she'd taken attendance, she started right in telling us what we were going to do this year.

"We're going to study the most interesting thing in the room," she said. We all looked around, wondering what that could be, and she laughed.

"Ourselves," she said. "And the species we belong to—mammals."

I put up my hand. She squinted at her seating chart. "Rosie Maxwell—you have a question?"

"Will we study sea mammals?" I asked. "Like whales?"

"Of course," Ms. Pingree said, giving me her big, friendly smile. "Are you interested in the ocean?"

I nodded. "I'm going to be a marine biologist," I blurted. I'd never said that out loud before, except to Mama, but Ms. Pingree made me feel brave.

"Here we go—Maxwell the mad scientist," someone chortled. Without even turning around, I could tell it was that loudmouth Bromjay.

Ms. Pingree ignored him. "Perfect!" she told me. "You'll be just the person to help me organize our class trip. I hope we'll go on a whale watch, and to Sea World, if we can raise enough money."

Whale watch? Sea World? Leah and I glanced at each other and grinned. Things were looking up, and we'd been in the room only fifteen minutes. Suddenly the loudspeaker came on.

"Ms. Pingree, excuse me for interrupting," said the box on the wall. "Would you please send Rosie Maxwell to the office?"

Everyone hooted except Leah, who looked sorry for me. I practically crawled out from my seat. How could I be in trouble already?

I hurried down the hall with my head down. Luckily, I didn't see anyone I knew. Miss Danders, the principal, was waiting in her doorway. She pulled me into her office and pointed to the wooden bench where kids hang out when they're in trouble. "Sit down, Rosie dear," she said.

Dear! What makes grown-ups think they can call you "dear" when they don't even know you? I perched on the edge of the bench, wishing she'd close the door so no one could see me.

"I'm terribly sorry to bother you," Miss Danders said, "but I'm afraid your brother's gone missing."

"Huh?" I said, feeling stupid. Why was this happening to me?

Her smile was completely fake. "Dan went to his classroom before school and met his teacher. Then he said he had to go to the bathroom, and he never returned."

I stared at her. "I just saw him," I said. "He came to my room, right before the bell rang, and then he went back upstairs."

"Did you actually see him go up?" Miss Danders asked.

"Well, no." My neck prickled, and my hands felt sweaty. Where could Dan be?

"We've searched the building," Miss Danders said. "I thought you might know where he's gone."

"Uh-uh." Geez, first my mother, now the principal—everyone expected me to be in charge of Dan. I was only in fourth grade! I checked the clock; it was time for math, my best subject. "Can I leave now?"

"Just a minute." Miss Danders gave me this beady look, and I turned away to keep myself from staring at the mustache above her lip. "If you were Dan, where would you go?" she asked.

"I don't know," I said. "Didn't you call my mom?"

"Of course; we tried her right away," Miss Danders said, "but no one was home. Do you know where she is?"

"She's probably changing the baby or working in her studio," I said, and then I remembered that Mama had said something about taking Clara to the doctor. "You can call my dad at the high school."

Miss Danders nodded. "We left a message there. I'm sure he'll call back soon."

"Listen, if Dan's lost, they'll want to know." Man, oh man. How did this lady ever get to be principal?

"Don't worry, hon, we'll keep trying."

Hon! I stomped to the door, but Miss Danders put her hand on my shoulder. "Don't get upset, dear. I have an idea." She picked up the microphone on the secretary's desk. "Why don't you speak to Dan over the PA system? If he's here in the building, I'm sure he'll come out when he hears your voice."

I stared at her. "You mean—talk to everyone in the *whole building?*" I gulped. Really, I couldn't think of anything more embarrassing—unless one of those dreams came true, the ones where you showed up at school in your underwear.

"Sure!" she said, in her syrupy voice. "It's fun!"

I could tell that Miss Danders and I had different ideas about fun. She turned on the microphone, flipped a switch on the secretary's switchboard, and said, "Excuse me children. This is Miss Danders, your principal. Welcome back to Park Street School!" She blabbed on and on about learning and having a positive attitude. Just when I was hoping she'd forgotten about me, she added, "We've had a little mix-up this morning. One of our new first-graders, Dan Maxwell, seems to be lost. Daniel, if you're listening, your sister has something to say to you." She shoved the microphone into my hand and whispered, "Go ahead."

"Uh—" The mike felt cold and heavy in my hands. "Dan. This is Rosie." I nearly jumped out of my skin when my own scratchy voice boomed from the loudspeaker outside the office. "Dan, go back to your classroom right *now*," I ordered, trying to make my voice sound deeper—and it did! All of a sudden, I decided Miss Danders was right; this could be fun. Before I could stop myself, I blurted, "And now, students, guess what?" I tried to make my voice come from the bottom of my stomach so everyone would listen. "Are you ready for this? Today we'll have . . . hot fudge sundaes for lunch! With cherries and whipped cream on top—all you can eat!"

I didn't get a chance to say any more because Miss Danders grabbed the microphone from my hand and switched it off. Two red spots were glowing on her cheeks as if she'd smudged lipstick on them.

"That's quite enough, Rosie Maxwell," she said.

"We don't tell lies on the public address system. I'm going to write you up for a detention. Will you do that for me please, Ms. Jones?"

"Certainly," the secretary said, and she shook her head at me, pulling out that pad of pink paper that meant trouble. I didn't wait to see or hear any more; I dashed out and ran down the hall. Kids in every class were yelling "Yay! Ice cream!" and teachers were shushing them.

When I got to my room, I slid behind my desk. "Big shot, big shot, Rosie is a big shot," Bromjay sang softly under his breath. Everyone else chattered until Miss Danders's voice came on the loudspeaker again. "I have to apologize about Rosie Maxwell's teasing," she said, her voice clinking like ice cubes. "Unfortunately, we do not have hot fudge sundaes today. But she *was* telling the truth about her brother Dan. Daniel Maxwell, if you can hear me, please go back to your classroom right now."

"No ice cream!" the class groaned.

"Quiet down, please," Ms. Pingree said. I hunched in my chair and wouldn't look up, even though Leah was trying to pass me a note. Ms. Pingree handed out our new math books; she stopped beside my desk and frowned at me. "That was an unfortunate way to start the day," she said. "I hope your behavior improves."

I sighed. So Ms. Pingree was like other teachers after all—full of big words and stuck-up attitudes. I opened my book, but I couldn't concentrate. I was mad at Dan, and worried, too. Usually, he was so quiet we hardly noticed him. Why did he have to go and do something dumb, wrecking my first day in school? Would someone in my family always be in a mess? And speaking of messes, what would my parents say when they heard about my detention?

I felt like bees were buzzing around in my head, asking questions I didn't want to hear. What if someone had kidnapped Dan? Would that be my fault? I studied the clock, waiting for the big hand to jump forward. I didn't move. Maybe I'd be stuck here forever, waiting for time to pass. My hair would turn white. I'd need a cane . . .

Ms. Pingree woke me from my daydream. "I'll put our first math puzzle on the board," she said. "If you have two pet rabbits, and they have six babies . . . and then, each of those rabbits grows up to have six babies . . ."

Usually, I love puzzlers, but this one made me think about the rabbit they have at the School in the Canyon. "Oh, no!" I gasped, suddenly realizing where Dan must be.

The class giggled, and Ms. Pingree's eyebrows raised up into little upside down V's. "Is something wrong, Rosie?"

"Yes—I mean, no." I squirmed in my seat and jammed my hands under my legs, trying to keep them still. Why, oh why, did I ever tell Dan he could go back to the School in the Canyon? Didn't he know I was joking? The more I thought about it, the more I was sure that he'd walked right out the front door and wandered off across the big five-way intersection, not looking where he was going. He wouldn't notice if the crossing guard was gone; he'd be too busy studying the cracks in the sidewalk or the feathery branches of the palm trees.

I thought of Mama saying she could count on me. My eyes got watery. I rubbed them hard, but they started to itch, so I rubbed them again.

"Is something wrong, Rosie?" Ms. Pingree asked.

I shook my head, but she hovered over my desk, looking like someone's worried grandmother. "Your eyes are terribly red," she said. "Are you all right?"

Everyone stared at me. This was definitely the worst day of school in my whole life, and fourth grade had barely started. "I'm fine," I gulped. "It's just my allergies."

"Ah." Ms. Pingree looked interested. "What are you allergic to?"

My family, I wanted to say, but I just mumbled, "Lots of stuff."

Leah rolled her eyes, and I ducked my head.

"I think you'd better see the nurse," said Ms. Pingree. "Here's a pass." She gave me a wooden block that said "Nurse" on it. "Have her check it out."

I left the classroom again. If only the earthquake would come now—the big one they always talked about on television. When a huge crack opened under my feet, I'd sink to the bottom of the ocean. A gray whale would adopt me, and I'd live happily ever after.

My sandals squeaked on the shiny waxed floors. I stopped before I turned the corner to the nurse's office. Miss Danders hadn't come to tell me Dan was found, so he must still be gone, right?

The door at the end of the hall was open, and the sun was shining on the swings in the yard. Without even thinking, I dropped the pass on the floor, ran out the door, across the playground, and down the street. I went faster and faster, looking over my shoulder in case someone from school was racing after me. When a police car went by, I ducked behind a tree, but the woman driving didn't even turn her head.

It took forever to get across the five-way intersection. I pushed the button, waited, jumped up and down, got more and more jittery, pushed the button again. Finally, all the cars slowed down, then stopped. When the "Walk" sign flashed, I hurried across and kept running all the way to my old school.

3. Jinxed

The kids were outside, building forts with big blocks, pushing trucks, and making motor noises. Katie ran up to me; her cheeks were red, and her pants were covered with green paint. "Rosie," she said. "Why are you here?"

A couple of little girls stopped playing and stared at me. Their faces were grubby from digging in the sand. "Come here," I whispered to Katie, dragging her away from everyone. I was all out of breath. "Where's Dan?"

Katie cocked her head to the side. "He's in first grade," she said, as if I didn't know that already.

"He's supposed to be," I said, "but he ran away."

"Then he's probably at home," Katie said. "That's where I'd go." She stared at me a second, then ran off with her friends.

I looked around quickly. Dan *must* be here. He wouldn't go home, would he?

Rachel came outside, holding a little boy's hand. "Why, Rosie." She looked surprised. "Is something wrong? Did you come here by yourself?"

My eyes were burning, and sweat trickled down my face. When Rachel put her arm on my shoulder, I bit my lip to keep from crying. "Dan got lost at school," I said. "I thought he might be here." I glanced all around while I was talking. I had this terrible sinking feeling in my stomach.

"I don't think so," Rachel said, "but we can look." All the little kids were standing around us now, staring at me. Rachel called to Jen, the other teacher, and asked her to phone my mom.

"She's not home," I said quickly.

"Just to make sure," Rachel said. Then she gathered everyone into a circle. "We're going to play hide and seek," Rachel explained, making it sound like a game. "We're looking for Rosie's brother Dan."

"He's my brother, too," said Silas, coming up to me. He pushed back his yellow hard hat and blinked. "Dan's at the big school."

"No, he's not." I was feeling hot and mad and much too old to be standing in this little kids' playground filled with sandy trucks and bulldozers. "Dan's lost," I told him. "I think he ran away from school."

Silas and Katie both looked as if they might cry, and Rachel put her arms around them. "Don't worry, twins, he'll turn up. He's probably off investigating something. First one to find him gets to serve the snack!''

Typical nursery school kids: they thought it would be *fun* to take the snack tray around. They squealed and started running across the playground. We looked in the cement tunnel, under the jungle gym, in the bushes. We searched the school closets, the cupboards, and the bathroom, but Dan wasn't there. Jen came back and said there was no answer at my house, and the phone at my school was busy.

Rachel made everyone sit in a circle on the classroom rug, asked Jen to read them a story, and took me into her office.

It sure was different from Miss Danders's room. There was a cozy chair and a big table with stacks of picture books on it. Rachel put her hand on the phone, then looked at me. ''Rosie, dear, does anyone know you're here?''

I shook my head. Leaving Katie at the beach was nothing, I guessed, compared to the trouble I'd be in over this one.

''I think I'll try the school again,'' Rachel said, putting her hand on the phone. ''They'll be terribly worried.''

In one second, I decided anything would be better than facing Miss Danders a second time. ''*Please* call my house first,'' I begged. ''Maybe my mom's come home.''

Rachel nodded. "All right." She looked up the number, dialed, and gave me the phone when it started to ring.

To my surprise, Mama answered right away, and when she heard my voice, she shrieked, "Rosie Maxwell! Where are you? We were ready to call the police!"

I started to cry. "I'm fine, Mama," I said, sniffling. "I'm at the School in the Canyon, looking for Dan—but he's not here."

Clara was screaming close to the phone, sobbing so hard she made a little trilling noise like a clarinet. Mama didn't say a word for one long minute, and then she said, "You children are driving me absolutely crazy. Of course Dan's not there; he's at the Park Street School, and that's where *you* should be, young lady." I could feel her eyes flashing at me right through the telephone. "Now would you please tell me what's going on?"

I gave Rachel a desperate look. There was no possible way I could explain what had happened. I handed her the phone and huddled in the chair, hugging my knees. I was never going to get out of this mess—never.

Finally, Mama and Rachel sorted things out. When Rachel hung up, she smiled and said, "What a mix-up!' Miss Danders called your mother, and she went over to the school. They found Dan in another classroom or something. I'm not sure I understand, except that everyone's been looking for *you* for the last hour. Now that your mother knows where you are, she'll call the school and explain.''

''And then she'll pick me up?'' I asked.

Rachel shook her head. ''Clara's upset from having a shot, so your mother asked if you could stay here and help me out. Also, she doesn't want you to cross that big junction without a guard.''

Of course, I'd already crossed that intersection alone, but I decided not to mention it to Rachel. I remembered a book about a boy who had such a terrible day he decided to move to Australia. Maybe he and I could get together and have a club. Only kids who had miserable days could get into it.

Rachel was still talking. ''After lunch, you can walk the twins home.''

I could hear Bromjay now. ''What's the matter, Maxwell, decided to go back to preschool?'' And Shirley would have some snide comments to make.

I was stuck. I spent the rest of the morning wiping up spilled juice, reading stories to little kids, and helping them dress up in old costumes. Finally, it was time to leave. Rachel shook my hand as if I were one of the parents and said, ''Thanks, Rosie, you've been a big help. I guess you've had lots of practice taking care of little kids!''

Too much practice, I thought. I took the twins' hands and started up the street. The closer we got to our house, the more worried I became. What would Mama say? When she was angry, you'd wish you lived even farther away than Australia—Mars, maybe. Silas and Katie chattered and giggled as if nothing had happened.

4. Family Blues

Just as I thought, Mama was mad as a hornet. Her eyes sparked, her chin stuck out, and she put her hands on her hips. Silas and Katie disappeared as soon as they saw her.

"Rosie Maxwell!" she snapped. "What on earth got into you? You scared me to death."

"It was Dan!" I cried. "Miss Danders told me he was lost."

"Dan was not lost," Mama said in her most dangerous, quiet voice.

"Yes he *was!*" This was so unfair I couldn't believe it. "Miss Danders called me to her office and made me announce it over the loudspeaker to the *whole school!*"

Mama's mouth twitched. "From what I understand, you also had some fun with the microphone." For a second, I thought she might smile and forget the whole thing, but no such luck. "Your announcement worked," Mama said. "Dan was in the wrong classroom. When he heard your voice, he went right back to Mr. Cutting's room.''

I stomped my feet. ''But no one told me! I thought he was kidnapped or something.''

Mama frowned. ''Well, that was an unfortunate mistake, but I still don't understand why you ran away.''

''I didn't!'' I yelled. ''You told me to take care of Dan. You just don't understand. Now my whole class will laugh at me, and I'll have to stay in from recess— all because you made me take him to school!''

Mama took a deep breath. ''Rosie Maxwell, you *know* you did something wrong. You don't just run off like that, without telling anyone. And I can't believe you crossed that big street without a guard. I want you to go to your room and think about it for a while. I expect a good explanation before dinner tonight.''

I ran upstairs and slammed my door so hard that I woke Clara, who was asleep in my parents' bedroom. ''Too bad for you,'' I said, stuffing the pillow against my mouth. ''It's all your fault, anyway. If you'd never been born, Mama would have taken Dan to school the way she was supposed to.''

It made me feel even worse to have thoughts like that. I was hot all the way to my stomach. I took the Do Not Disturb sign off my bedpost, hung it on the doorknob, and stayed in bed all afternoon. After a while, I heard Silas and Katie having fun out in the yard, and later, Dan got dropped off and started playing with them.

I got up, went to my desk, and wrote this short note: "Mama, I didn't do anything wrong. You told me to take care of Dan. Signed, Rosie Maxwell." I folded the note, put it outside the door, and got back in bed. I heard someone stop and pick it up, but the footsteps just went away again.

When Dad and Shirley came up the walk, I buried my head under my pillow, pretending to be asleep. After a while my door opened.

"You could knock," I said, keeping my head covered. I'll suffocate, I thought; then they'll be sorry.

"Rosie." Dad pulled the pillow away. "We need to have a little talk."

I knew all about Dad's "little talks." They were kind of like his lectures on how to do hard math problems. He'd drone on and on, putting you to sleep. I peeked out from the pillow and groaned. Dan and Shirley were in the room too. "What is this, a party?" I asked.

"It's my room, too," Shirley sniped. "In case you forgot."

"Now Rosie," Dad said, "I know you and the Professor here had a tough day. Why don't you tell me about it?"

"Geez," I said. "You sound like a teacher."

"I *am* a teacher." Dad's voice was as tight as a rubber band. When I didn't answer, he said, "How about you, Dan—want to explain what happened?"

"There's nothing to tell," Dan said. His face was quiet and calm, like nothing had gone wrong. I stuck out my tongue at him, then turned toward the wall. He'd messed up my whole day, and he wasn't even sorry.

"What's this about ice cream sundaes?" Shirley asked.

"None of your business," I snapped.

"Sounds like you've both got a bad case of school blues," my dad said.

"What are those?" I mumbled into my bedspread.

"It's when school stinks," Shirley said. "Like it did for me today. I found out nobody in seventh grade wears surfer T-shirts."

"So—don't wear them," I said, rolling over. "At least you won't have detention for the rest of the year because your little brother decided to get himself lost."

"Now, now," Dad said. "Hold on. Let's talk about school blues for a minute. I had them myself this morning."

"You did?" Shirley asked.

"Sure," Dad said. "I was so homesick for Clara in third period that I left the kids in study hall and went to the office to call your mom. When I got back, students were throwing spitballs, and one girl was climbing out the window. Luckily, my classroom's on the ground floor."

I crossed my arms and glared at Dad. How come he was homesick for Clara but not the rest of us?

But Shirley obviously thought it was funny. "Dad—really? Did Mr. Jones find out?"

"Of course not," Dad said. "I know how to stay out of trouble with the principal."

I waited for him to say, "Not like some people I know," but he didn't, thank goodness.

"Well, I don't have school blues," Dan announced in his high, squeaky voice. "I *like* school."

"What?" I demanded. "Then why did you come whining to my room to tell me school stinks?"

"Because," Dan said.

"Because, why?"

"Now Rosie, don't screech."

Oh boy, now Mama was in the room too? Forget having privacy in this family. "What is this, a trial or something?" I demanded.

"Let your brother talk," Dad said.

I sighed, and Dan took a deep breath. "I could read all the first-grade books," he said, "so I decided I was ready for second grade."

I glanced at Shirley, and she raised her eyebrows. Now *that*, I thought, is a good one. "Didn't the second-grade teacher notice?" I asked.

Dan shook his head. "Uh-uh. Some kid named Alex Petrie was sick, and I took his seat. The teacher thought I was him."

"And then?" Dad asked. His eyes were twinkling.

"I heard Rosie on the loudspeaker, so I went back to

my classroom. I told Mr. Cutting what was wrong, and he said I could keep on reading chapter books if I want. Plus, he's going to teach me to write my own stories and make them into books like Mama's. So I think I'll like school after all.'' Dan crossed his arms and gave us this proud smile, as if he'd just graduated from college.

"Well, that's one down," Dad said. "So Rosie got you to go back to your classroom, but she didn't even know it."

Shirley was staring at me. "Miss Danders made you talk to the whole school?" She actually sounded sympathetic.

"Yeah. It wasn't so bad." I thought of how deep my voice sounded and how big I felt, knowing everyone was listening.

Shirley frowned. "I hope I never have to do that at my school," she said.

Dad stood up, squeezing my knee. "So, do you have school blues, Rosie-Lou?"

"No," I said. "I have family blues."

Mama and Dad both laughed.

"It's not funny," I said. "No one else comes from such a messy family."

"What's wrong with us?" Dan asked. "I like our family."

"So do I," Mama and Dad said together.

"I like it too. Most of the time," Shirley added.

"You wouldn't understand," I said. "You're the oldest."

"So what?" Shirley said. "That means you always have to do things right. It's tiring."

I stared at my sister. I'd never thought about it that way.

"It's true, our family gets a little wild," Mama said, "but it can be fun. Your dad and I grew up in small families, and we thought they were lonesome," she added. "That's why we had so many children."

That's a dumb reason, I thought, but I didn't say so. "I bet you don't know what it's like to make so many mistakes in one day," I said.

Mama laughed. "Of course we do, Rosie. Your dad and I make mistakes all day long."

I stared at her. Since when? I wondered. Dad smoothed my bedspread. "We'll make a fresh start tomorrow," he said. "You can just go to school and take care of Rosie Maxwell—no one else."

I squirmed in my bed, pushing my feet against the end. "There's just one thing," I said, glancing at Mama, then looking away fast. "I got detention for making up that story on the loudspeaker."

Shirley laughed. "Detention's nothing in grade school. You miss one recess. Everyone passes gum and notes around. And if you're lucky, Miss Danders will forget. She usually does."

I sat up. My stomach was growling; I realized I'd

missed lunch. The day was almost over, thank goodness.

"What about it?" Dad asked. "A new beginning in the morning?"

"Okay," I said finally. I looked at Dan. "Tomorrow, you stay in your classroom, all right?"

"I will," he said.

"You too," Dad said to me.

"You too," Mama said, poking Dad.

Dad laughed. And the next day, we all did.

PART IV
FIRE!

1. Boring Saturdays

The third week of school was over. It was supposed to be fall, but it was so hot you could almost hear the chaparral crackle in the canyon. It was too hot to practice gymnastics, even in the shade. I sat in the kitchen on Saturday afternoon, sliding the salt shaker back and forth across the table.

"The wind's from the desert," Mama said. She pulled the shades to keep the sun out. "When the Santa Ana blows, we all get parched."

"What's 'parched'?" Silas asked. Since he started talking, he wanted us to explain every word.

"It means everything gets dried out," Mama said, licking her lips. "Can't you feel how dry your hair is?" She laughed, tapping Silas on the head. He was wearing his hard hat, of course. "Guess you can't tell, with this thing on."

"My eyes hurt," Dan complained. He was whittling a stick with his jackknife, leaving shavings on the floor.

"That's because of the smog," Mama said. "The wind blew the smog away from the desert, and now it's sitting over us."

I thought about an ugly yellow cloud creeping around our house like a robber. "Smog is boring," I said. "Saturdays are boring. We never do anything exciting now that Clara's here."

"I like Clara," Katie said, pouting. "You're not being very nice."

I stuck out my tongue at her. How could I be nice when I didn't feel nice? My mouth was all dry inside, as if I'd just swallowed a lizard. I poured some salt on the table and made tracks with my fingernail, then wrote my name in it.

"Don't," Mama said, taking Clara out of her baby-seat. I stood up and climbed the inside of the door, bracing myself against the frame with my bare feet, using my hands to haul myself to the top.

"Don't, Rosie," Mama said again, without even looking at me. Did she have eyes under her hair?

"It's good for my legs," I said, but I dropped to the floor anyway. It was too hot to argue. I landed in a crouch, and something yellow fell out of my shorts. I bent over to pick it up. It was the poster about the gymnastics meet. I smoothed it out on the table. It must have been through the wash at least once; it was so faded I could hardly read it.

"What's the date today?" I asked.

Mama didn't answer. She was holding Clara up over her head, cooing at her and laughing when Clara gurgled back. Clara drooled right on Mama's blouse, but Mama didn't seem to care.

Dad and Shirley came into the kitchen. Shirley's lips were bright pink; she'd probably been using Mama's lipstick—without permission, naturally. Dad was carrying his trumpet and a bundle of music for band practice. "What's the date?" I asked him.

"The twenty-first," Dad said. "Why?"

I squinted at the crumpled paper. "Wow! That's when the gym meet is happening," I said. "It's tonight." I took a deep breath. "It would be so neat if we could go."

"Hmmm?" Dad mumbled. No one else was paying attention to me, of course. Katie and Silas were racing around the kitchen. Katie was shooting Silas with a purple squirt gun. He ducked under the table and scooted out again, with Katie following him. "Can I have friends over for dinner?" Shirley asked.

"Listen," I said, but no one did. I felt invisible. I jumped onto a chair and waved my arms. "Be quiet!" I yelled.

Mama and Dad put their hands over their ears. "Rosie . . ." Dad warned.

"No one ever listens to me!" I waved the paper in front of Dad's nose. "Look," I said. "There's a national gymnastics meet, right in L.A., tonight. Can we go?"

"I don't think so," Dad said, but Mama set Clara in her lap and said, "Let's see." She studied the poster a second. "Gymnasts from all over the country—that would be exciting for you to watch, wouldn't it, Rosie?"

I nodded, holding my breath. Shirley glanced at the paper, then tossed her braid over her shoulder. "How boring," she said. I clenched my fists so I wouldn't hit her and waited. Mama and Dad were looking at each other.

"Well . . ." Dad began.

"It doesn't cost much," I said quickly. "Kids under twelve are free. Since Shirley thinks it's boring, she could stay home." I glanced at Shirley; she crossed her eyes at me and flopped into a chair. "Please, Mama?" I begged. "I've never seen top gymnasts before."

Dan closed his knife. "We never go anywhere," he said. "Not even the movies."

"A trip! The movies! Whee!" Katie and Silas came screeching into the room; they leaned on Dad, panting like puppies. "Can we go?" Of course, they didn't even know what we were talking about. I guess they figured anyplace we went would be more exciting than here. They were sure right about that.

"There's just one thing," Mama said. "I was planning to work on my rain forest book later, after your dad gets home from the football game—"

"We could baby-sit right now," I interrupted,

"couldn't we, Shirley? Then we could all go out tonight."

"Well . . ." Shirley said.

"Come *on*," I begged.

"Rosie's right," Dad said. "We could use a little entertainment. I'll be back as soon as the band finishes playing at halftime; I can help out then. Be a sport, Shirl."

"And it's not as if I'll be far away," Mama said. "After all, my studio's right out back."

Shirley and I raised our eyebrows at each other. Whenever Mama was in her studio, she might as well be on Mars.

"Okay," Shirley said, with a big, heavy sigh. "I don't have anything better to do. But I'll only watch Clara. Rosie can take care of everyone else."

"Fine," I said. That sounded easy to me.

Katie pushed her lower lip out. "I don't need to be baby-sitted," she said.

"Neither do I," said Dan. He looked at Dad. "Can I come with you to the game?"

"Sure," Dad said. "But you'll have to watch the band rehearse before the kickoff."

"Forget it," Dan said. "Your band hurts my ears."

Mama laughed, and Dad held his glasses up to the light, then rubbed them on his shirt. "Gee, thanks, everyone," he said.

I ignored him; I was starting to get excited. I beckoned to Dan and the twins. "We'll do something much more fun than football," I said. "We'll play a great game—then we'll go to the meet. It will be fantastic!" I jumped off the chair and flipped upside down, walking on my hands. When my legs toppled me over, Clara squealed, and I tickled her tummy. "You're going to your first big gym meet, little chubster," I said.

Mama smiled. "Why Rosie, it's nice to see you cheerful about something for a change."

I grinned back. I wanted to say, "It's nice you're paying attention to me for a change," but I didn't want to spoil everything.

Dad opened the door and leaned out, sniffing the air. Mama laughed. "You look like a dog," she said. "What are you doing?"

"There's a big fire over in Agura. The air smells a little smoky. All the hoses are hitched up, if you need them." He pointed at the sign on the wall. "Don't forget, everyone," he said, "the number of the fire department is right by the phone."

"Don't be silly," Mama said. "Agura's miles from here. Besides, we don't have fires in Copper Canyon."

Later, we always remembered her saying that.

2. A Dragon Breathing Fire

Mama finished nursing Clara and put her down for a nap. She hurried back through the kitchen, her eyes dark and shiny. "Shirley," she said, "listen for the baby—don't spend your whole time on the phone." She twisted her hair up on top of her head. "You can give her a bottle when she wakes up, and check her diaper. Call me if you need me. And you kids, do what the girls say."

Dan scowled. "Rosie and Shirley are *not* my bosses," he muttered, but Mama just smiled. Her eyes already had that faraway look that meant she was thinking about her drawings. When she opened the back door and stepped out, I imagined she was walking into her book and that our backyard was filled with bright, colorful insects and long, squiggly snakes.

Shirley went right upstairs. I was pretty sure she was going to disobey Mama the first chance she got, but I decided to ignore it. I looked at Dan and the twins. "What'll we do?" I said.

"Play," Silas said.

"Play what?" I asked.

"Dress up," Katie said.

Dan groaned. "I'm going to finish my comic," he said, picking one up.

"Wait a minute," I said. "Let's play knights and dragons. Katie, you and Silas can be the courtiers."

"What's coort-ears?" Silas asked.

"The people who wait on the king and queen and do their bidding," Dan explained. He'd just finished reading a chapter book about King Arthur and his Knights of the Round Table.

"What's bidding?" Silas asked.

Dan held his place with his finger. "That means you have to do what the king and queen tell you," he said. He flipped the comic back open.

"Please, Dan, don't read," I begged. "It's more fun if everyone plays. We can get stuff from the trunk. Besides," I added, thinking fast, "you always have good ideas, from the books you're reading."

"All right." Dan sighed. "I've read this comic before anyway."

We went into the family room, opened the heavy black trunk Dad used at college, and pulled out a purple cape, some silver high heels that belonged to Grandma, a plastic sword, and lots of hats, belts, and wigs. I dug into the bottom. "Hey, here's my favorite Halloween costume!" I showed them a silky yellow dress. "My princess outfit—I remember when I wore that." I tried to put it on, but it wouldn't even slide over my shoulders. "Darn," I said, "it doesn't fit anymore."

"I could be the princess," Katie said. I held the dress up to her, but the skirt flopped on the floor.

"It's much too big," I said. "You'll trip."

Katie pouted. "Then what can I be?"

"The dragon," I said. "You can be fierce."

Katie got down on all fours, waggled her rear end, and growled.

"Good," I said. "You'll be a great dragon. We'll have to fight you with all our might." I looked at the dress, then at Dan. "Guess what?" I said. "It's just your size."

Dan backed away. "No!" he yelled. "I won't dress up like a girl. I'm the king that slays the dragon."

"*I'm* the king," I said, waving the sword and jabbing it through the air. "Or the queen. I'm the biggest. And there's always a princess who's rescued from the dragon."

"So why can't *you* be the princess?" Dan asked. "You're a girl. Boys are princes and knights; they rescue ladies just before they get eaten by dragons."

"Not in my game," I said. "This time, the queen is the biggest and strongest."

"Dan, you can be a smart princess," Katie told him. "Figure out how to trick me, the dragon."

Dan's eyes flickered; he liked being called smart. But then he shook his head. "Forget it," he said.

I ran my tongue over my lips. "If you'll wear the dress, just for an hour, I'll give you my whole set of Nancy Drew and Hardy Boy Mysteries."

"No way," Dan said. "I'm not wearing a dress."

"I'll give you the ten dollars from my piggybank," I said. "You can buy a couple of books with it."

Now I'd got him. Whenever he begged Mama and Dad for new books, they always said they didn't have enough money.

"Okay, okay," Dan said finally. He took off his shirt and pulled the dress over his head. It fit perfectly. He looked at himself in the mirror and giggled. "The golden princess," he said, smoothing the skirt down over his shorts. "I need a crown."

"And some lipstick and long hair," I told him, pulling out a wig with yellow curls. "Here," I said, "you can have curly hair, like me. I'm going to make a crown, too, and a shield."

"Hey," Dan protested, pushing the wig off, but Katie and Silas danced around him, saying, "Leave it on! It looks good."

"This is weird," Dan said, but he kept the wig on his head.

"I need a dragon suit," Katie said. "Silas, what are you going to be?"

"A coort-eer," Silas said.

"Come on," Katie said, "let's get stuff from our room."

"Be right back, okay, guys?" I called, but the twins didn't answer.

Dan and I found brown paper, scissors, and magic markers. We went upstairs to Mama and Dad's room, tiptoeing so we wouldn't wake Clara. Dan went to Mama's dresser, borrowed an old lipstick, and smeared it on his lips. He climbed on the end of Mama and Dad's bed, so he could see in the mirror. He giggled. "I wish Andrew was here," he said. "He'd laugh."

I poked around in Dad's drawer until I found a big heavy belt I could use to hold up my sword. Just then, Mama poked her head in the door. "Rosie," she said softly, "will you be all right if I run down the hill to the art shop? My red acrylic's all gone. Tell Shirley. I'll be back in a jiffy."

"Sure," I said. Dan sat down real fast, and I grabbed Mama's lipstick, holding it behind my back. But she didn't even notice what we were doing: the heels of her boots clicked as she hurried along the hall and down the stairs. I waited until I heard the door slam, then dug into Dad's shirt drawer for cardboard to make the shield and crowns.

Dan and I went downstairs to the family room. We had our crowns all decorated and the shield cut out when I realized Katie and Silas weren't around.

"Oh no," I said, "where are they?"

The house was quiet; that was a bad sign. I put on my crown and hurried down the hall behind Dan. A big bag of flour was sitting on the kitchen floor right next to the table. The top was ripped open and mounds of flour were all over the place. There were heaps on the floor, the table, and the counters.

"Oh boy," Dan said, pointing at the kitchen tiles, "they even walked in it."

A line of little white footprints went through the kitchen, across the living room rug, and out onto the cement patio. We followed the tracks, running. "Katie! Silas!" I yelled when I saw them. "What are you doing?"

The twins were white from their eyebrows down to their sneakers. It looked as if Mama had dumped Clara's baby powder on their heads and shirts. Katie smiled at us. Her pigtails stuck straight out, and the tip of each one was white, as if she'd dipped it in paint. She squirted water from the hose into a bucket full of flour while Silas stirred.

"We're making cement," they said. Flour puffed up into their faces; Silas coughed.

"That's not cement," Dan said, "it's paste."

"It's cement," Silas said. "White cement."

We stared for a minute. Then I asked, "What's it for?"

"For the castle." Silas pointed to the stack of red cardboard blocks the twins used for building houses and forts. "We're going to cement the blocks into a castle. So the walls won't fall down. Then the dragon can't get us," he explained.

"But Katie," I said, "I thought you were the dragon."

"Uh-uh," said Katie, stirring. "Silas and I are knights. We're going to fight the dragon with you. It's coming to get us. See?"

She pointed toward the mountain at the top of the canyon. A soft puff of smoke floated across the sky. Dan and I stared with our mouths open. We looked at each other.

"It's the dragon breathing fire," Katie said.

At first, there were just wisps of smoke, like steam. Then a gust of wind blew hard, making Mama's wind chimes clatter and clang against the side of her studio, and the smoke whooshed into a black cloud.

"That's not a dragon," I said. "It's a brush fire."

Katie and Silas looked at each other. Their eyes got rounder and rounder, like dark buttons. "Will our house burn down?" they asked at the same time.

I didn't answer. The cloud oozed toward us like a black monster. When a giant orange flame burst over the top of the ridge and licked the tiny trees, we all screamed.

"We'd better get Mama," Silas said, grabbing my hand.

I blinked at him, suddenly remembering. "Mama's not here," I whispered.

Katie started to cry. "Where is she?" she wailed. "What if we get burned up?"

"I want Mama," Dan whimpered. "And Dad." He rubbed his eyes hard, trying not to cry.

"So do we!" Silas and Katie wailed. Everyone huddled close to me. I took a deep breath and touched the crown on my head. If I was going to be the queen, I'd have to be in charge.

"Let's pretend," I said, taking a deep breath. "Let's pretend the dragon is coming. What should we do?"

Katie held up the hose. "Spray him?" she sniffed.

"Right," I said. "Silas and Dan, you're the knights defending the castle—our house. You can spray it with water."

"Now?" Silas asked.

"If the fire comes," I said.

"No," Dan said. "I read in the newspaper that people get their houses all wet *before* the fire comes."

"Yeah," Silas said, grabbing the hose from Katie and waving the nozzle around in the air. "And they go up on roofs, too. I saw them on TV." He aimed the hose at the dining room windows and twisted the nozzle. "Go 'way, dragon!" he yelled. The water spurted against the windows and made dark streaks on the white wall.

"Spray the whole house," I told Silas. "Get everything wet. I'll call the fire department."

"I'll get the other hose," Dan said, and ran toward the garage, tripping over his skirt.

"What about Clara?" Katie asked.

Clara. And Shirley. Good grief. I'd forgotten all about them.

"And Rufus," Silas said. "If we run away, we have to take Rufus."

"Whatever," I said, and ran for the house.

"I have to get the crawl doll," Katie cried, scurrying behind me. "I'll pack all our stuff." I zoomed into the kitchen so fast, I skidded in the flour and fell on my knees. I scrambled up, really scared. What if Mama didn't come back?

3. *Fire in the Canyon*

I picked up the phone, studying the number on the wall, and started to dial. Someone was talking. "Shirley!" I yelled. "Hang up!"

"Get off the phone, creep!" she said.

"No!" I screamed. "There's a fire!"

"Don't kid," Shirley ordered.

"Yeah," her friend said, "you should never kid about fires."

"I'm not!" I was crying now, I was so mad. "Look out the window, idiot, if you don't believe me! Shirley, I'm going to scream until you hang up."

"Creep!" she said again and slammed down the phone. As I was dialing, I heard her run across the floor upstairs, and then cry, "Help! Mama!"

I gripped the phone. A lady answered on the first ring. "Fire!" I yelled. "There's a brushfire up here!"

"Who is this?" the lady asked in a cross voice. "Is this a crank call?"

I tried to make my voice sound more grown-up.

"This is Rosie Maxwell," I said, talking slowly even though my heart was beating a hundred miles an hour. "I live in Copper Canyon. There's a fire on the mountain." I looked at the sign taped on the wall. "My house is one mile up the road from the stop light," I told her, just the way Dad had written it.

"Now, now, little girl," the lady said. "I'm sure your parents would be very angry if they knew you were playing tricks on the fire department."

"It's not a trick!" I yelled. "There's a fire, and all the houses are going to burn up if you don't send someone." Why didn't grown-ups ever believe kids?

I heard a crackling noise on the phone, and then a man's voice calling out, in the background. "There's a report of smoke, sighted near Copper Canyon. Any other calls, Marge?"

Marge must have been the lady I was talking to because I heard her say, in a muffled voice, "There's a little girl on the line, claiming her canyon's on fire."

A man's voice came on the phone. "Who is this, please?" he asked.

"Rosie Maxwell," I said, peering out the window. The smoke was getting taller and taller, reaching up into the sky. "I live at 2929 Copper Canyon Road, and there's a big fire on the mountain. It's coming this way."

"Better let me talk to your mom or dad," the man said in a deep voice.

"They're not home," I said, and my voice started

quivering. "Please hurry, or our house will burn up."

"Calm down, honey," the man said. "We'll be there before you know it. Are you all by yourself?"

Honey. Why were grown-ups always calling me that? "There are *six* of us kids," I yelled. "Hurry, please! And bring a big truck!"

Suddenly, Clara screamed bloody murder. I hung up the phone and ran upstairs as fast as I could. "Please, fire, go somewhere else; don't burn our house down," I prayed, panting. I thought about fire drills at school, and how they made everyone line up and stand outside the building. Clara, I thought, and Shirley. I had to get them into the yard, fast. But what if the fire came down the road? Then what?

I hurried into Mama and Dad's bedroom. Clara's head went back and forth on the sheet and her face was bright red. Shirley was sitting in a chair by the wall, wiping her face. She was soaked all the way down her front.

"The firemen sprayed me!" Shirley whimpered. She sounded like Katie, not someone who's twelve and knows everything.

"WAAAAH!" Clara screeched. When I went to pick her up, a stream of water hit me in the face and splashed across Mama and Dad's bed. Clara was sopping wet. I jostled her in my arms and peeked out the window. The sky was black, and some gritty ashes floated past. Was the fire department here already? No, it was Silas; he was holding onto the hose, spraying the outside walls, and squealing. I couldn't tell if he was yelling because he was excited or scared.

"Silas, stop!" I screeched down at him. "You're spraying the inside of the house."

"Oops," Silas said. He whirled around, making wide circles on the grass like a sprinkler.

"Tell Dan to close the windows," I yelled at him. I slammed the window shut and jounced Clara. She was bawling her head off. "Hush," I said, "it's all right." I felt like a stupid grown-up, saying it was all right when it wasn't all right at all; it was terrible. I patted Clara's back but she wouldn't stop crying. Shirley huddled in the corner. Her face was white, like she'd smeared it with paste.

"Do something!" I said.

She covered her eyes and croaked, "Where's Mama?"

"She went to the art store," I said. "You're supposed to be taking care of us."

Shirley hugged her knees and rocked back and forth. "I can't," she whispered. "I don't know what to do."

Good grief, was everyone going nuts? "Go pack your bag," I told her. She still didn't move, and all of a sudden, I smelled this yucky smell. "Uh-oh," I said to Clara. "You promised you wouldn't do this to me, not while Mama and Dad are gone."

I put Clara on the bed, got a diaper and a clean

jumpsuit and when I came back, Clara had rolled almost to the edge of the bed! Boy, was I freaked. I put her back in the middle, unsnapped her suit, and held my nose.

"Yipes!" I yelled. "Gross!" Why, oh why, did I ever say I'd baby-sit? It was getting dark as night outside, and it was still the middle of the afternoon. From far, far away, I heard a siren wailing on the Coast Highway. "The fire trucks are coming," I said.

Clara hiccuped and waved her little arms and legs. She seemed excited about the trucks.

"Peew!" I said, unpinning the diaper. "You're a mess." Every time Mama or Dad had changed Clara's messy diapers, I'd gone somewhere else. Now I wasn't sure what to do. "Shirley," I begged, "can't you help me?" But Shirley was clutching the windowsill as if she were trying not to fall out. I folded up the diaper, grabbed all the pillows on the bed, and made a wall around Clara. She was happy to be naked; she kicked her legs and made circles with her arms, batting herself in the face with her fists. I ran to the bathroom with the diaper, left it on top of the toilet, and found some diaper wipes.

"Peewy," I said, wiping Clara's bottom. "Pew, pew, pew."

Now I could hear more sirens. The phone was ringing, but no one was answering it. I tried to pin Clara's diapers. No matter what I did, the material bunched up and the diaper was crooked. Why couldn't Mama and

Dad use Pampers, like everyone else? "Never mind," I said, pushing her feet into the legs of her rubber pants. "We've got to hurry." Clara just smiled and gurgled at me like everything was fine.

After I put her in a clean suit, I grabbed some more diapers, some shirts and a blanket, and the tiny stuffed bear she likes to chew on. "Shirley!" I said, nudging her, "don't you want to pack your stuff? We have to be ready when the firemen come to get us."

She didn't answer. Was she deaf? I ran to our bedroom, laid Clara on the rug and grabbed my backpack from under my bed. I threw in a picture of Leah and me on Santa Monica pier; a Mexican blouse Grandma bought for me on Olivera Street; the whale poster from my wall; and a model of a bottlenose dolphin. Then I took a giant duffel bag out of Shirley's closet and stuffed it with some of her clothes, her roller skates, and all the clips and ribbons she puts in her hair. I heard sniffling. Shirley was standing in the doorway, crying.

"Come on, Shirl. We're going to be okay." I actually gave her a hug, but it just made her cry harder. "Take your bag," I said, as if I were Mama and she were my little girl. Shirley stared at me, then finally moved, dragging the duffel bag downstairs. I followed her, holding Clara. I had a hard time, carrying the baby and my backpack. Clara's head bobbled against my shoulder.

Dan was slamming windows. I set Clara in the carriage and pushed her out the front door. Cars were racing down the canyon. Some of them had beds tied on top. Mrs. Stone went by in her old car; all kinds of stuff was dangling out of her trunk. Then Chad Nelson zoomed past in the pink van, with the donkey's head sticking out the side window. I wondered if all their chickens and rabbits were in there, too. Should we try to hitch a ride with someone? No, the fireman had told us to stay right here.

I didn't want to look up the road, but I couldn't help it. Orange, yellow, and red flames were dancing on top of the mountain; the fire was burning in three places. Black smoke was billowing everywhere. Clara started to cough, and Katie came rushing up to me, holding the crawl doll. Her face was all streaky and white.

"Where's Mama?" Katie cried. "Why doesn't she come back?"

"She will," I said, even though I was starting to get really worried. "Did you pack stuff for you and Silas?" I asked.

Katie nodded, pointing to a big box on the sidewalk. It was mostly full of toys and stuffed animals. I was about to tell her we'd need more than that if our house burned down, but suddenly a patch of something red came floating through the air and landed on the grass right near us.

"A spark!" I yelled, stomping on it. "The fire's here."

Dan and Silas came running. "There are sparks all over the yard," they cried.

"What'll we do?" Katie asked. Everyone was looking at me, even Shirley, who was leaning against the front door, half in and half out of the house, like she didn't know where to be.

"How should *I* know?" I asked.

"Cuz you're the queen," Katie said.

I stared at her and took a deep breath, pulling myself up tall the way queens do to show they have royal blood. "Look, the queen says the fire is here, and we have to fight it. Come on, everybody, listen up. We're going to save our house."

4. The Maxwell Fire Brigade

I started giving orders. This would be fun, I thought, if we weren't about to get burned up.

"Katie, go tell Shirley to come outside," I said. "Silas, bring the hose over here!" I stomped on another clump of burning grass. Silas dragged the hose toward me. His face was bright red, and his eyes bugged out. He sprayed the grass until it stopped smoking. More sparks were blowing toward us on the wind; some of them drifted down the canyon, but a big one landed on our house.

"Dan!" I yelled. "Help me get the ladder. We'll have to spray the roof."

"I can't get the dress off," Dan said, trying to pull it over his head. His wig fell on the ground.

"The zipper's stuck," I said. "Here." I yanked, but it wouldn't budge. "Tuck it into your shorts." He did, and we ran to the garage, dragging the big ladder outside. It was heavy. "Shirley!" I yelled. "Silas!

Come help us.'' We were huffing and puffing, trying to haul the ladder around the corner to the front yard. Katie came running out the door.

"Shirley won't come outside," she said. "She's too scared."

What was this, the new Shirley? I didn't have time to worry about her. "Okay, ask her to call the firemen again and tell them to hurry. She can probably remember how to use the phone, at least. And then stay with Clara, near the door."

Katie hurried back inside, her chubby legs pumping. Dan and I set the ladder against the low part of the house, over the kitchen. I looked up. The roof seemed far away. "Aren't you scared to go up there?" Dan asked.

I was, for a second. But then I thought of the rings, high above the gym floor at gymnastics. This was just the same, only there weren't any mats if I fell. Better not to think about that. I gritted my teeth and scrambled up the ladder onto the roof, holding the nozzle of the hose.

Standing on the sloping shingles, I could see the road twisting through the canyon. A siren shrieked, and then another one started wailing. Finally, I saw the flashing lights. "The fire trucks are coming!" I yelled, and twisted the nozzle. "Silas and Dan, spray Mama's studio!" I called.

Dan ran down the path and closed Mama's windows

while Silas dragged the other hose over and aimed it at the walls. I sprayed the kitchen roof until the shingles were wet and shiny. My eyes burned; the sky was smoky and bits of burning brush were flying through the air. Sometimes they landed right near my feet. I knew there must be sparks on the big roof over our bedrooms, but I didn't know how to get up there. It was too high. I tried lifting the hose over my head, but the water still didn't reach the upper roof; all I did was give myself a shower.

"Mama, please come home," I whispered. The first fire engine went racing by, then another one.

"Stop! Stop here!" Silas yelled, waving his arms, but the trucks kept right on going.

"They have to go where the fire's burning," I called.

I sniffed and looked up. Something was smoking on the big roof above me. If we didn't hose it down, the house might catch on fire. But how could I get up there? I looked at the drain pipe, curving over the roof and down the wall beside me. I grabbed it and tried to shake it, but it didn't budge; it seemed sturdy. Would it hold my weight? The gymnastics coach always said I was light and wiry.

I took a deep breath, tucked the hose nozzle into my heavy belt, and shimmied up the pipe. It was slick and cold, but it had grooves in it that were pretty easy to hold onto. I used my leg muscles, the way I did climbing the big knotted rope in our gym. In a few minutes, I scrambled over the lip of the roof and stood up carefully. Shingles were smoldering right beside me. I turned the nozzle on them, hard. The hose was tight, but the water reached. In a minute, the fire was out.

Then I dared to look into the canyon. It was filled with cars, trucks, vans, and fire engines, streaming past in both directions. A man was on his roof across the street, spraying it just the way I was. I felt big and proud for a second, until Dan called, "Rosie, how are you going to get down?"

Before I could figure that out, a police car came wailing up the canyon. It zoomed by, and right behind it was our station wagon, driving faster than Dad drives on the freeway. It screeched to a halt in front of our house—and Mama jumped out! She came racing up the walk as if a thousand monsters were after her, screaming our names at the top of her lungs.

"Mama!" I cried, waving my arms. "Mama, it's okay! We're all right!"

Dan and Silas ran to her and threw their arms around her waist, almost knocking her down. Katie struggled along the sidewalk, pushing Clara; she was so short the carriage handles were over her head. Then Shirley burst out of the house, yelling her head off. Mama hugged everyone quickly. "My babies," she sobbed. "My babies. Are you all right?" She counted, gasped, and cried, "Rosie! Where are you? Where's Rosie?"

Mama noticed I was missing! I was so happy I didn't even mind being called a baby. I leaned over the edge of the roof. "Mama," I called, "I'm up here!"

Mama squinted and looked up, shading her eyes. "Rosie Maxwell, where on earth—"

"On the roof," I yelled, sitting down so my feet could dangle over the edge. I waved. "Look up!"

Mama craned her neck at me, then leaned against the side of the house as if she might fall over. "Rosie, get down this minute," she ordered, and then she said, real fast, like a car reversing directions, "I mean, no, don't move. Stay right there. Just what do you think you're doing?"

"There were sparks burning the shingles. I put the fire out."

Mama opened her mouth, then shut it. I thought she'd lose her temper again, but instead she called up, "Well, aren't you smart."

"Is our house going to burn down?" Katie asked.

"Not if Rosie or I have anything to say about it," Mama announced.

Boy, was I glad to hear Mama talking that way! I whooped and turned the hose on again, spraying water all over the place. I'm afraid some of it dribbled onto Mama.

"Rosie, hold still!" Mama ordered. "I'm coming upstairs to rescue you. If I can't get you down, we'll call the fire department."

I had to laugh. "Mama, who do you think called the fire department in the first place?"

But Mama had disappeared. Shirley threw her head back so she could see me. "That's not very smart," she said. "You could fall off."

"Well, I see *you're* back to normal," I answered. Then I moved, and fast. There was no way Mama or anyone could get to this place from inside the house. And I was *not* going to get rescued by some stupid fireman with a ladder, like a cat stuck in a tree. I tossed the hose down onto the kitchen roof, stuck my glasses into my pocket, grabbed the drainpipe and swung myself out over the edge. I slid down as slowly as I could. My feet dangled over the empty air for one long, awful second, then I swung off the pipe and dropped onto the hot shingles. "Ouch," I said, rubbing my hands; the metal had burned my palms. I picked up the hose, sprayed myself, and then the roof again. A window opened next to me and Mama stuck her head out.

"Rosie, my goodness, how did you get down?"

"I climbed," I said. "Mama, the fire's coming closer. Please get your stuff together. We don't have much time."

She cocked her head. "Rosie, you're obviously in charge, and you're right. Boy, am I glad you were here today." She ducked inside. In a minute, she was rushing to the car, lugging a big suitcase. "We have to be ready to leave at a moment's notice," Mama called up to me. "If anything starts to really burn, yell bloody murder. Shirley, are you all right now? Keep an eye on Clara, that's my girl. Dan, come with me."

They ran to her studio. Boy, the world was really upside down if Mama was asking me to yell my head off. I kept spraying the roof and watching the flames. They seemed to jump from one part of the mountain to another, like kids playing leapfrog.

Mama stumbled out of her studio carrying a huge black portfolio full of her pictures; it bulged like a fat man whose pants are too tight. Dan dragged out a bag full of books and art stuff. They put everything in the car and hurried back into the house. I coughed, and suddenly I smelled something burning right near me. I put my hand to my head. My crown was on fire! I pulled it off and drowned the fire with the hose, then put it back on. Fire or no fire, I was still the queen.

Mama ran past again. "Get off the roof now, Rosie," she said, huffing and puffing. "I want you all to stick close to me." I sprayed everything one last time and climbed down the ladder. Mama rushed around, throwing things into a big box by the front door. I saw Dad's clarinet, a junky pile of mail, some photo albums, Mama's illustration from the cover of her first book, Clara's pacifier, and some other stuff I didn't think was that important. Mama was moving faster than a VCR movie speeded up.

"Keep Clara right beside you," she told me. "We

may have to abandon everything. The fire looks pretty bad.''

Dan started to cry, but I pushed him out the door. ''Shut up,'' I said. ''We don't have time to bawl. Carry some stuff to the car.''

We lugged more boxes down the walk. Katie followed us, holding the crawl doll. ''Our house is going to burn up,'' she sobbed.

''Don't be silly,'' I said, even though I thought she was right. One, two, then three more fire trucks raced up the canyon with their sirens wailing. Silas came running down the walk, carrying Rufus in his cage.

Chop, chop, chop; thwack, thwack, thwack! Two helicopters flew so low over our house that we ducked. They zoomed sideways up the hill. A police car pulled up beside us with its red lights flashing as Mama stuffed another box into the station wagon.

''Getting out, ma'am?'' the policeman asked.

''What does it look like?'' Mama snapped. Shirley sucked in her breath, and I was scared; would the policeman arrest Mama for talking that way?

''I'm loading my belongings,'' Mama said, ''but I'm not leaving until my husband comes home.''

''We'd like to evacuate everyone now,'' the policeman said.

''What's 'vacuate?'' Silas whispered, but I hushed him. Mama had her hands on her hips.

''I'll decide when it's time to leave,'' Mama said.

"My entire career is in my garage, and I'm not about to feed it to the flames."

The policeman was smart. He didn't try to argue with Mama; he just shrugged his shoulders. "As long as you're prepared to pull out when we say it's time," he said. He glanced at Rufus, sniffed, then gave us a funny look and drove further up the canyon.

That's when Mama seemed to notice us for the first time. She stared at my crown, then at Dan, with his dress poking out of the bottom of his shorts, then at the twins, with flour all over their faces. "You certainly are a sight," she said, and laughed. We watched her face carefully; was everything going to be all right? But then she glanced at the mountain, and her eyes got dark again. "Please," Mama whispered, as if the fire could hear her, "don't take our house."

We huddled close together. I shivered even though the air was as hot as an oven. Mama wasn't supposed to look so scared.

5. The Queen of Copper Canyon

For a little while, the flames got taller and taller on top of the ridge. Fire trucks kept racing up the road, and more cars came down, loaded with stuff. Silas and I took turns spraying the house while Mama and Dan packed boxes in the car. Katie kept Clara happy by bouncing toys in front of her and wheeling her up and down the living room. Shirley stood around, waiting for someone to tell her what to do next. No one said anything about Dad, but we were all worried; every time we put another box in the station wagon, we'd look down the road, waiting for our little red car to show up.

All of a sudden, the sirens stopped wailing; it was so quiet, we could hear the crackle of the flames high above us. We stood still, staring at the smoke. Instead of blowing toward our house, it was billowing the other way!

"Mama, look!" I yelled.

Mama stood still on the sidewalk, licked her finger, and held it in the air. "The wind's changed," she said. "They've got it under control."

"Will our house be saved?" I asked.

"Of course it will," a voice said.

Dad! I recognized his voice, but the man didn't look like our father. His face was black, his glasses were held together with a safety pin, and his shirt had a big tear under the arm. "Hi, kids," he puffed. He was all sweaty and hot.

"Dad!" we yelled, hugging him. "Where have you been?"

He took off his glasses and wiped his eyes. Was he crying? "They wouldn't let me past the barrier down below," he said. "So I had to go up higher and come into the canyon from the side streets. The fire got pretty close. I'm afraid I had to leave the old car."

"Is it burned up?" Silas asked.

Dad shrugged. "I don't know. The police wouldn't let me drive in here, so I had to abandon it."

"What's 'bandon?" Silas asked.

"He left it there," Dan said.

"A few people higher up lost everything," Dad said. "The Nelsons' barn is gone, although I guess they got their animals out."

"They did," I said. "We saw the donkey in the van."

Dad nodded, as if donkeys rode in Volkswagens

every day. "I was frantic," he said. "I didn't know where you were, or if you were all right. I kept calling, but the phones don't work."

He hugged Mama, and she started to cry. The rest of us stood and watched the oily clouds billow up into the sky. Everything smelled smoky and bitter. The fire was burning farther away now, but the whole mountain was black. "It looks like the mountain died," I said.

"It did," Dad answered softly, "but when the rains come this winter, it will turn green again. The chaparral grows quickly after a fire."

My heart felt sad for the mountain, for the Nelsons, who lost their barn, and for the people who didn't have anyplace to live.

Finally Mama said, "These kids did a great job while I was gone."

Dad stared at her. "Gone? Where did you go?"

Mama explained how she'd run out of red paint. "The police gave me that same line about how I couldn't come up the canyon," she said, grinning. "I just drove right past the barrier."

Dad laughed. "That must have surprised them."

We all giggled. I could just imagine Mama gunning the car and wheeling around the sign while the policemen yelled at her.

Dad looked at Shirley. "So, did you hold down the fort?"

Shirley stared at the grass and shook her head.

"Rosie told us what to do," Katie said, puffing out her chest. "We were playing dragons and knights. When the dragon came to burn us up, we killed him with our magic water."

"The dragon was on the big roof," Silas said. "Rosie was brave. She climbed way up there and sprayed out his fire!" He picked up the hose and whirled around, stomping his feet and imitating me.

Dad looked up at the top of the house, then down at me. "Above our bedroom? How did you get up there?" he asked.

"I climbed the ladder and then the pipe," I said. "It was like gymnastics."

Dad shook his head. "That's the craziest thing . . ."

"The roof was burning," Dan said. "She saved our house."

Dad's face got red. I didn't know if he was going to laugh or cry. Instead, he grabbed me and hugged me so tight, I couldn't get my breath.

When he let go, Shirley sniffed. "I was such a chicken," she said. I actually felt sorry for her, for the first time in my life.

"I was scared, too," I said. "Really, Shirl. I got mad and rushed around so I wouldn't have to think about it. And when I climbed up high, I was petrified. I took my glasses off so I couldn't see the ground."

"You didn't sound scared," she said. "Just bossy, like me."

Everyone laughed. Then Shirley touched my hair. "Everyone will *really* notice your mop now," she said. "It looks like you dyed it."

I touched my head. "Really?" I asked.

Mama smiled. "It's the new style," she said. "Red and silver, like your crown."

"Like the fire," I said. Mama sat down on the grass, and we all flopped down beside her.

"Mama, will you be mad?" Katie asked suddenly.

"Mad?" Mama asked.

"Mad about what?" Dad asked.

"The cement," Silas said.

"It's all over the kitchen," Dan said.

"And everywhere else," I said. "But they didn't mean to," I added. "I mean, it was my idea to play castles."

Dad and Mama looked at us as though they didn't know what we were talking about. "Cement?" they asked. "Castles?"

I touched Katie's braids, then Silas's nose. "Flour and water," I said, "makes cement to hold the castle together."

Dad smiled. "Oh, I thought you were smudged from fighting the fire."

"We are!" Silas said. He grabbed a hose and turned it on. Instead of spraying the house, he got us all wet, even Clara. We laughed and shivered, and then Dad asked, "Are we still going to the gymnastics meet?"

"I don't want to," I said quickly.

Dad's eyebrows went up. "Why not, hon?"

I lay back on the wet grass and took a deep breath. "I think I've had enough gymnastics for one day."

Mama and Dad laughed. "I bet," Mama said.

I stood up and looked around at everyone; there was Dan in his yellow dress with lipstick all over his face, the twins covered with flour, Dad and Mama with their sooty faces. Even Shirley was a mess, her hair tangled up and her eyes all runny and red. I knew I must look pretty weird too, with my hair turning wild colors under my soggy crown. I laughed. "Remember when I said we were a messy family, and everyone got mad at me?" I asked.

Mama nodded, grinning. "We *are* pretty messy today, aren't we?"

Clara started to fuss. I took her from Mama and bounced her up and down. "You know what?" I said. "It doesn't bother me so much anymore."

Clara drooled on my shirt. I handed her back to Mama. Then I whirled into two cartwheels, did a back flip, plunged into a forward roll, and finished with a handstand. My glasses and crown flew off into the grass.

"Show off," Shirley muttered, but I didn't care. I was Rosie Maxwell, Queen of Copper Canyon, firefighter, gymnast, and member of a Number One Crazy Family. And for once, I was proud of it.

Family